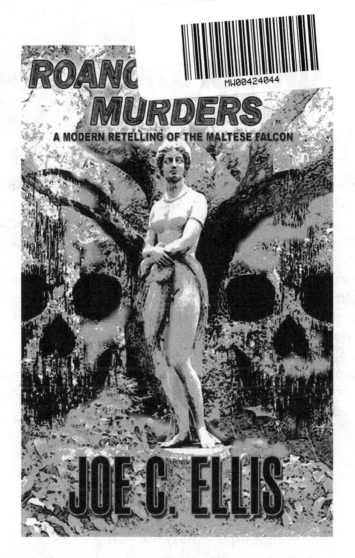

ROANO
MURDERS

A MODERN RETELLING OF THE MALTESE FALCON

JOE C. ELLIS

A novel by

Joe C. Ellis

BOOKS

Weston Wolf- Outer Banks Detective Series

Upper Ohio Valley Books
Joe C. Ellis
71299 Skyview Drive
Martins Ferry, Ohio 43935
Email: **JoeCEllisNovels@comcast.net**

PUBLISHER'S NOTE

Although this novel, Roanoke Island Murders, is set in actual locations, the Outer Banks of North Carolina and Roanoke Island, it is a work of fiction. The characters' names are the products of the author's imagination. Any resemblance of these characters to real people is entirely coincidental. Many of the places mentioned in the novel—Buxton Village Books; Downtown Books, the Cameron House Inn, the Burrus House Inn, Manteo, NC; Buxton, NC; Hatteras, NC, are real locations. However, their involvement in the plot of the story is purely fictional. It is the author's hope that this novel generates great interest in this wonderful regions of the U.S.A., and, as a result, many people will plan a vacation at these locations and experience the beauty of these settings firsthand.

CATALOGING INFORMATION
Ellis, Joe C., 1956-
Roanoke Island Murders
A Modern Retelling of the Maltese Falcon
by Joe C. Ellis
ISBN 978-0-9796655-9-2
1.Outer Banks—Fiction. 2. Roanoke Island—Fiction
3. Mystery—Fiction 4. Suspense—Fiction
5. Manteo, NC—Fiction 6. , Hatteras, NC--Fiction
7. Buxton, NC—Fiction 8. Detective—Fiction

Books by Joe C. Ellis

Book 2 – Weston Wolf Outer Banks Detective Series
The Singer in the Sound

Book 3 – Weston Wolf Outer Banks Detective Series
Kitty Hawk Confidential (August 2021)

Outer Banks Murder Series

These are stand-alone novels and can be read in any order.

The Healing Place (Prequel to Murder at Whalehead)
Book 1 – Murder at Whalehead
Book 2 – Murder at Hatteras
Book 3 – Murder on the Outer Banks
Book 4 – Murder at Ocracoke
Book 5 – The Treasure of Portstmouth Island
Outer Banks Murder Series 5-Book Set

OUTER BANKS MURDER SERIES by Joe C. Ellis

Prequel - The Healing Place

Murder at Whalehead

Murder at Hatteras

Murder on the Outer Banks

Murder at Ocracoke

The Treasure of Portsmouth Island

ROANOKE ISLAND MURDERS

A Modern Retelling of The Maltese Falcon

Chapter 1

Angie Stallone opened the frosted door and peered into Detective Weston Wolf's office.

"Yes, Angel," Wolf said.

She was a tanned girl of medium height whose white pantsuit clung to her athletic body with wonderful flow. Her eyes were bright blue in an innocent face. She shut the door behind her and crossed her arms. "There's a lady waiting to see you. She says her name is Carolyn Couch."

"I presume she wants to talk to a detective?"

"That would be my educated guess."

"Is she good looking?"

Angie scowled. "You'd probably give her a nine out of ten."

"Really? Give me a minute and then send her in."

Angie stepped outside the office and closed the door.

He snatched his cell phone from his desktop, pressed his thumb on the access button, tapped the camera app and touched the two arrows to switch to the back camera. He examined his face to make sure he looked presentable. His prominent jaw had a white scar near his chin that contrasted with the three-day growth of beard. He flared his nostrils to make sure no hairs had grown since he last plucked them. Wetting his fingertips, he smoothed his rust-colored brows that shadowed his deep-set hazel eyes. His sandy hair appeared jumbled like an unruly pile of discarded yarn. With his right hand he raked his fingers through his locks to make sure they flowed more smoothly over his pointed ears. He sat the phone down and eyed the *To Protect and Serve* tattoo on his forearm. The words were entwined with handcuffs. He chuckled. *A reminder of the high ideals of my youth.*

Angie opened the door. "Are you ready?"

Wolf smiled, picked up the phone and checked his teeth. "Send her in."

She glanced across the outer office. "Miss Couch, Detective Wolf will be delighted to speak to you now."

"Thank you," a breathy voice said. The woman entered and approached Wolf's desk hesitantly. Her dark brown eyes gazed at him, as if trying to disrobe his soul.

She was tall, thin and angular with high, firm breasts. To Wolf she looked like the models on the covers of the magazines in the grocery stores. A black mini dress, clasped in the middle with a loose tie, failed to cover much of her long legs and milky shoulders. When she smiled, her bright red lips created a crescent of perfectly ordered teeth. Her black hair, cut in a short, shaggy style, framed her light complexion.

Wolf stood and motioned to one of two old wooden armchairs in front of his desk. He was six feet two inches tall, perhaps four inches taller than his potential client. He prided himself in his 185-pound physique, keeping his weight close to his linebacker college days. He wore a gray golf shirt with a white shark logo on the breast pocket and black gaberdine pants.

"Thank you," Miss Couch purred and perched herself on the edge of the chair.

Wolf plopped down on his padded swivel chair, spun and leaned forward, facing her. He smiled, nodded and placed one hand flat on his desk next to a half cup of cold coffee. The dark brown crumbs of a cream-filled cupcake were scattered around the cup. He quickly swiped the crumbs off the desk with a few flicks of his hand.

"Sorry about the mess. One of my many weaknesses — junk food. I've got a whole box of them in my drawer here."

The woman eyed him uneasily. A seagull screeched just outside the window, and distant waves rumbled along the shore sixty yards beyond the house. She shifted her gaze to the window.

"I know what you're thinking," Wolf said. "This old beach bungalow doesn't appear to meet very high standards as far as a detective agency goes, but I assure you, Miss Couch, my partner and I strive for excellence in all the services we offer."

"I'm sure you do," the black-haired beauty said. She crossed her legs, redirected her eyes to Wolf and placed her leather shoulder bag in her lap.

Wolf took a deep breath and rocked back in his chair. "Now, Miss Couch, what can I do for you?"

"I—I—I was hoping . . . That is I—I thought maybe . . ." Her lower lip trembled, and then she bit it with those glistening teeth. Her dark brown, almost black eyes, blinked several times and focused intensely on him.

Wolf smiled, gripped the edge of his desk and scooted forward, "Now, now, Miss Couch. You can trust me with whatever is on your mind. Everything is confidential. Why don't you start at the beginning."

"That would be Charlotte."

"Charlotte? Is that a friend or relation?"

"No, that's a city."

"Of course, the Queen City. You do mean Charlotte, North Carolina?"

"Yes. That's where we grew up, my best friend Emma Ritz and I."

"And what brings you to the Outer Banks? A vacation?"

"Yes. We've been coming here in August for the last several years."

"I see." Wolf rubbed the three-day stubble on his chin. "This is about your friend, Emma?"

She bobbed her head. "Five days ago we arrived at the Sandbar Bed and Breakfast just north of Jockey's Ridge."

"Ah, yes, not far from here."

"You were the closest detective agency I could find. There's not many on the Outer Banks."

"No. Not much demand. So what happened? Is your friend safe?"

She glanced around the room and twisted the strap of her handbag. "I don't know."

"So this is a missing persons case?"

"Yes . . . I mean no. On our first night here she met a man at a bar, the Lucky 12 Tavern. He's renting a beach house on the oceanfront. She went to his place that night and left me to fend for myself."

Wolf sat up straight. "And you haven't seen her since?"

She blew out a long breath. "I've seen her a few times. She has stopped by the room at the bed and breakfast, but . . . but . . . she's different now."

"Different how?"

"I think she's been mesmerized by this man. Maybe even brainwashed. His name is Frank Fregiotto. He's . . . he's . . . odd. I think he's dangerous."

"Maybe they're in love. Falling in love can do strange things to a person."

"I believe he's after her money. She's well-to-do. I can tell he's a conman. She wasn't the prettiest gal in the bar. Far from it. With his looks he could have hit on any one of those women. But he chose her. She was wearing a diamond necklace and a Hermes quartz watch. Those timepieces go for more than five thousand dollars. He noticed it immediately."

"I see. So you're worried about her. You want me to keep an eye on her and make sure nothing unusual happens. Perhaps I can do a background check on this Fregiotto and get a better idea about the kind of man he is—his past, police records, that sort of thing."

"Yes but . . . I—I was hoping . . ." She touched her fingers to her lower lip. Her fingernail polish matched the bright red lip color. "I was hoping you could do a little more."

Wolf adjusted himself in the chair by pushing down on the armrests and shifting his rear. "A little more in what way, Miss Couch?"

"This evening at eight I am picking Emma up for dinner. We're going to the Blue Moon Grill in Nags Head. I convinced her to pull herself away from Fregiotto to spend some time with me. He didn't seem to mind. He said he'd take a walk on the beach and then watch a baseball game on television to keep himself busy. I was hoping you could wait outside his beach house until we left and then confront him. Let him know that you've got an eye on him."

Wolf formed a fist with his right hand. "Maybe even scare him a bit?"

Her eyes widened. "Yes, if that sort of thing doesn't conflict with your business ethics."

Wolf's smile turned into a wide toothy grin. "Oh no, Miss Couch. No conflict at all."

She swallowed. "That's perfect. Maybe I can talk some sense to her when we're at dinner. Then I'll try to convince her not to . . ."

The office door swung open, and Miss Couch jerked like a startled cat.

"Sorry," the man said. He was dressed in a button-down forest green shirt and camouflage cargo shorts. "Didn't know you were meeting with a client." He was a few inches shorter than Wolf, a few pounds heavier and few years older.

As he backed out, Wolf said, "No problem, George. Come right in. I'd like you to meet Miss Carolyn Couch. This is my partner, George Bain."

Bain entered and nodded to the woman. He had thinning brown hair, gray around the ears. His thick neck and bulging biceps offered evidence of his dedication to weightlifting.

Miss Couch smiled at him and lowered her eyes, nervously fidgeting with her purse strap.

He ogled the woman from the top of her head to the tip of her toes and back again. With a bawdy smile, he looked like he had just heard a dirty joke.

"Miss Couch is very worried about her friend Emma Ritz," Wolf said. "They were vacationing this week here in Nags Head. Emma met a man by the name of Frank Fregiotto at the Lucky 12 Tavern and has gone off with him."

"That's not nice," Bain said. "She left you by your lonesome down here? That wouldn't be any fun."

"I'm not worried about me. I'll get along fine. I'm worried about her."

"He's bad news?" Bain asked.

Her features tensed. "I think so."

"Miss Couch believes he's a conman," Wolf said, "out to get Emma's money. She wants us to check him out and let him know we won't let him get away with anything."

"I see," Bain expanded his wide chest. "Put a little scare into him."

"I don't think he'll scare easily," Miss Couch said. "He seems like the mafia type. I wouldn't be surprised if he carried a gun. If you approach him, please be careful."

Bain chuckled. "Don't worry about us, Miss Couch. We can handle ourselves."

Wolf glanced at Bain and smiled slyly. "This shouldn't be too hard. One of us will hang around outside of his rental this evening. After you pick up Emma, we'll see if he goes for a walk on the beach. That would be a perfect time to confront him."

"What does he look like?" Bain asked. "Tall, short, medium?"

"He's rather tall." She shifted her gaze to Wolf. "About your height. I'd say he's in his mid-thirties and a little over two hundred pounds. Very athletic looking, broad shoulders and all. He's got dark brown hair, medium length, and neatly trimmed sideburns. He has a Mediterranean look about him, very tan."

"How about his manner?" Wolf asked. "Is he forceful, laid back, friendly?"

"I would call it fake friendly. When he approached us at the bar the first night, he was very affable, but it didn't take long for me to see a sinister side below the surface. I wish Emma would have noticed it. I wouldn't be here right now if she had."

Bain grinned. "They say that love is blind."

"That must be true." She knotted her forehead. "Poor Emma. I hope one of you can save her from this heartbreak or at least prevent that cad from robbing her blind." She zipped open her leather shoulder bag and pulled out her wallet. "Will four hundred dollars cover everything?"

Bain raised his eyebrows. "That will be plenty. And I'll look after this personally, Miss Couch. You have my solemn promise that I'll take care of Mr. Frank Fregiotto for you." He reached and turned up his palm.

"Thank you so much." She placed four one hundred-dollar bills into his hand.

"You're welcome. And don't worry if you don't see me when you arrive. I'll be somewhere in the shadows."

"I understand." She gave them Fregiotto's address, thanked them again and departed.

Wolf closed one eye and pointed at Bain. "My, O my, you sly private eye. I've never seen you move so quickly to take a case."

"With a woman that beautiful, I figured I had to beat you to it. Besides, I'm good with damsels in distress."

"Let me remind you Detective Bain, you are a married man."

Bain frowned and held out his hands pleadingly. "Did you have to bring that up?"

Chapter 2

The familiar sound of his ring tone cut into Weston Wolf's half sleep. After the third ring he finally located his cell phone on the nightstand and managed to bring it to his ear. "Hello . . . This is Wolf, what's up? . . . Say that again. . . . He's dead?" Wolf rubbed the sleep out of his eyes. "What's the address? . . . Just north of the pier? . . . I see. . . . Okay. I'll be there in fifteen minutes."

Wolf glanced at the digital alarm clock on the bedside table: 2:00 a.m. He reached and toggled the switch on the nightstand light, squinting against the glare. The wind from off the ocean blew the curtains into the room. For mid-August it was a cool evening. He had hoped to get a good night's sleep, but that wasn't going to happen. He went to the window and gazed at the Atlantic Ocean. A full moon hung above the horizon, limning the white caps as they lapped the beach. He lifted the screen, stuck his head out the window and took a deep breath of the salty air. *Life just threw a helluva curveball. Dammit.* He turned his head to the left and peered along the shoreline. "The body's about two miles north of here. Yeah, that sounds about right . . . according to the address she gave us." He wagged his head in disgust.

The shoulder holster for his Sig Sauer semi-automatic pistol was slung on the bedpost. Focusing on it, he stood and stretched. He stepped over to the dresser, slid open the top drawer and selected a black t-shirt with the Wolf and Bain logo in yellow plastered on the front. *That'll have to be changed.* He funneled into the t-shirt, pivoted and strapped on the shoulder holster, making sure the gun was securely positioned. He stepped into his loosely fitting jeans and found a black nylon jacket hanging in his closet. After zipping up the jacket, he made sure the gun didn't bulge too much. He stuffed his wallet into his back-jeans pocket, grabbed his phone, swiped his car keys off the dresser and headed out the door.

Wolf's oceanfront cottage on East Hunter Street also served as the agency's office. The body was discovered just north of Jeanette's Pier not far from the address that Carolyn Couch had given them—Frank Fregiotto's rented beach house. The engine of his '69 Cougar rumbled as he slid to a stop before turning right onto Old Oregon Inlet Road. The street ran along the edge of the ocean and changed its name to Virginia Dare Trail after crossing East Gulfstream Road. Wolf often wondered why a street would change its name in the middle of town. Must have something to do with local history, he figured.

He pulled into the parking lot of Jennette's Pier and saw two Dare County sheriff vehicles, white Chevy Impalas with the Cape Hatteras Lighthouse logos on the doors. From there he hoofed it onto the beach where an ambulance flashed its red and yellow lights across the wide stretch of sand and dark ocean. Wolf cut over to the wet sand for firmer footing and hustled across the two hundred yards toward the ambulance. Ghost crabs lit by the moon scattered in every direction.

A small crowd had gathered, and a stocky deputy motioned the onlookers to back away and keep their distance. As Wolf zigzagged through them, the deputy put up has hands. "Wait a minute, buddy. Who said you could cut through here?"

"I'm Weston Wolf. Deputy Joel Thomas just called me."

"Oh, okay. I didn't recognize you in the dark." He thumbed over his shoulder. "You can go on through."

The ambulance's flashing lights backlit a few EMTs standing a short distance away. One of them held a flashlight on the body. To the left, Sheriff Dugan Walton and Deputy Joel Thomas crouched with their own light, inspecting something in the sand. Wolf drew closer to the body, and, sure enough, his partner George Bain lay sprawled akimbo on his back. His eyes were wide in a death stare, his mouth agape as if someone had just told him his dog got run over.

"Hello, Wes." The young deputy stood, holding a plastic evidence bag at his side. "I figured you'd want to see him before we moved the body." He was a baby-faced kid about twenty-four years old with brownish blond hair and a Kirk-Douglas cleft chin. He wore the typical gray law enforcement outfit and a black ballcap with the lighthouse logo. Wolf had crossed paths with him many times during the last two years on various investigations. He was an okay cop.

"Thanks, Joel," Wolf said as he leaned and took a closer look at the body. "Anybody know what happened?"

"Sure." Deputy Thomas said. "Somebody shot him right in the ticker. One shot's all it took as far as we can tell."

Wolf straightened and stepped toward the two lawmen. "What's in the bag?"

"A strand of hair," Deputy Thomas said. "That's all we've found so far."

"No cartridges lying around?"

"No sir."

"Hmmph. The killer must have met him right here. They faced each other. George always carries his revolver. He must not have expected the guy to be armed. They exchanged some words. The gunman raised the pistol and shot him right in the heart."

"Yeah," Sheriff Walton said with a gravely voice. He waved at the body. "There he fell." Walton was dressed in a black uniform and wore a double brim black hat. Red-orange hair sprang out around his ears and a thick brownish-red mustache covered his upper lip. He was broad chested with just a slight paunch, a seasoned lawman in his early forties. He wasn't Wolf's favorite person.

"Any idea who did it?" Deputy Thomas asked Wolf.

"Nope."

Sheriff Walton said, "You don't seem too bothered that your partner just went belly up."

Wolf shrugged. "Things happen. It goes with the territory."

"Uh huh," the sheriff grunted.

"Who discovered the body?"

"A young couple on a late-night beach walk," Deputy Thomas said.

Wolf stuck his hands on his hips. "That'll douse any plans for a passionate evening on the beach. Any other witnesses?"

Sheriff Walton waved at the people who stood near the other officer. "None of those rubberneckers know anything. We'll canvas the area to check for leads."

"Maybe somebody heard the shot," Wolf said.

The sheriff nodded. "Maybe. We haven't been here that long, but don't worry, we'll check it out."

"Do you want to take a closer look at him?" Deputy Thomas asked.

"No. I'll stay out of your way and let you do your work."

The young deputy grimaced. "We checked his gun. Just like you said, he didn't get a chance to fire it."

"Too bad. He should have known better."

"Another thing," Deputy Thomas said, "he had four one hundred-dollar bills in his wallet."

"Was he on a case?" Sheriff Walton asked.

"He was checking out a guy by the name of Fregiotto. Don't know much about him." Wolf gave them the same description of the man that Miss Couch had given him.

"Why was Bain tailing him?" Sheriff Walton asked.

Wolf tilted his head and gave him a tight-lipped smile.

"Come on, Wolf," the sheriff growled. "We need to know if we're gonna make any progress here."

"He might be a conman. I don't know much about him. Sorry I can't give you more than that."

"Yeah, right." Sheriff Walton snarled. "You never give much."

"You know the business. I'm under contract with a client. Don't try to corner me."

Walton expanded his chest. "Don't tell me what to do."

Wolf chuckled. "I'll stay out of your way if you stay out of mine. I'm heading across town to break the news to George's wife." Wolf turned and walked in the direction of the pier.

Deputy Thomas called out, "Sorry about your partner. I didn't know him that well, but I'm sure his loss will be difficult for you and his family."

"Thanks, Joel," Wolf said over his shoulder. "He definitely didn't deserve it."

When Wolf got back to his car, he pulled out his cell phone and called his secretary, Angie Stallone. She answered with a groggy voice.

"Sorry to wake you up in the middle of the night, Angel, but George is dead. Someone shot him on the beach near Jennette's Pier. . . . Keep calm now. . . . I need you to be a rock for me. . . . steady yourself . . . take a couple of deep breaths . . . I want you to visit Laura and break the news to her. . . No. You do it. You know it wouldn't be wise for me to talk to her. Tell her that I'll see her soon. Try to keep her away from the office. . . . Yeah. That's my girl. You're a true saint. I'll see you tomorrow. Goodbye."

When Wolf entered his bedroom, the digital alarm clock on the nightstand flashed 3:20. He zipped off his jacket and threw it on the bed. He yawned, stretched, unhitched his shoulder holster and looped it over the bedpost. *I need a nightcap.* He trudged into the kitchen, pulled a bottle of red wine from the cupboard next to the refrigerator and poured a tall glass. Leaning against the counter, he drank it down with several gulps and refilled the glass. He walked back into the bedroom and sat on the bed, slowly sipping. He stared out the window at the ocean and recalled his relationship with George Bain. The wine and the sound of the waves calmed his nerves. Taking his time, he enjoyed the second glass, savoring each sip. He and Bain got along okay. Their five-year partnership was somewhat successful, despite Bain's lack of good instincts and carelessness. *Too bad, that's what got him killed.* He glanced at the alarm clock — 4:20. *I need to get some sleep. Geesh. What a night.*

A hard rapping shook the front door. *No! She's the last person I want to see. Dammit. I told Angie to keep her away from me.* He lifted the empty glass and put it on the nightstand. *Oh well. I guess I have to bite the bullet sooner or later.* He stood, walked out of the bedroom and down the short hallway and then made a right toward the front rooms that served as offices. Through the frosted window of the front door he saw the shadowy forms of two people,

One of them pounded on the door again, and a man's voice shouted, "Wolf, are you in there!"

"I'm coming. Don't get your panties all in a knot." *It's not Laura.* Relief flooded over him. Wolf crossed the front office to the door and opened it. Deputy Joel Thomas stood smiling beside a disgruntled Sheriff Walton.

"Good morning, Wes," Deputy Thomas said.

"In my book it's not morning until the sun comes up."

"Sorry for the intrusion," Thomas said, "but we need to talk to you again."

"You friendly boys in gray are always welcome here." Wolf motioned to two plastic chairs against the wall near Angie's desk. "Take a load off."

The two lawmen squatted onto the creaky seats, and Wolf perched himself on the corner of the desk.

"Would you like a glass of wine?" Wolf said and grinned.

"No alcohol while we're on duty," Walton grumbled. Dark bags had formed under his eyes. With his bushy mustache he looked like a tired walrus.

"I should have taken that for granted. You boys always play by the book."

Walton glanced around the room with dispassionate eyes. "We have standards in our profession, not like this half-baked establishment."

"That's why I no longer put on the hallowed uniform, Sheriff. I couldn't play by your rules."

"No kidding," Walton grunted. "I've always taken that for granted."

"All kidding aside, what can I do for you?"

"Who said I was kidding," Walton grumbled.

Deputy Thomas smiled and clasped his hands. "Wes, did you get a chance to see Mrs. Bain and tell her about George's death?"

Wolf nodded. "Yes I did. It was a difficult visit to make, but I had to do it. She took it hard. I feel bad for the lady."

"You're damn liar." Walton leaned forward, elbows on his knees, his green eyes burning into Wolf. "We contacted Mrs. Bain, and she said your secretary stopped by and told her."

"Well, we work as a team."

"Yeah," Walton grumbled. "Team Me. Give the hired hands the tough jobs."

"Get to the point." Wolf's amiable expression hardened into deadpan eyes and a rigid jaw. "Why did you come here tonight?"

"What kind of firearm do you carry?" Sheriff Walton asked.

"I don't carry a gun. I hear they're dangerous. Of course, we have some here in the office."

"I want to see them."

"That's not a problem. First let me see your search warrant."

"So you don't want to cooperate with us?" Walton asked.

"I get the feeling this isn't a friendly visit."

Deputy Thomas frowned. "C'mon now, Wes. You know we're just trying to do our job. We didn't come here to yank your chain."

Wolf stood. "Well, then what the hell is going on? Get to the bottom line. You think you can come in here and grill me like a swiss cheese sandwich? I'll be damned if you can!"

Sheriff Walton stood and thrust out his chest. "Relax. Have a seat. There's no need to get contentious."

Wolf stiffened. "You don't tell me what to do in my own office. I'm not putting up with this crap. If you're going to treat me like a two-bit shoplifter, there's the door."

Deputy Thomas stood and held up his hands. "Wait a minute, Wes. We don't want to fight with you. We're just trying to find some things out."

"That's right," Walton said. "We want to know more about this Fregiotto. You practically told us to shove off when we asked about him. What are you hiding?" He raised his finger in front of Wolf's face. "I knew one day you'd make a wrong move, and today's the day."

Wolf smiled and relaxed. He took a step back and sat on the corner of the desk. "Everybody makes mistakes. I don't claim to be a Sunday school teacher. What have I done to upset you so much?"

"Who's this Fregiotto?" Walton growled.

"I told you everything I know about him."

"You told us next to nothing."

"That's what I know."

"Why was Bain on his trail?"

"Obviously, a client hired us to check him out."

"Who's the client?"

"You know I can't answer that question unless the client wants to be known."

Walton's eyes narrowed. "Let me remind you that this is murder. I didn't come here to play tiddlywinks with you. If you don't tell me who this client is, I'll go straight to the judge and get a court order."

Wolf waved his hand dismissively. "Listen, Mr. Tin Star, I don't start spouting privileged information when you say, 'Talk or else.' The last time a policeman made me cry was back in fifth grade when I got caught soaping windows."

Deputy Thomas sat back down on the plastic chair and gazed up with wounded eyes. "Please, Wes. Give us a break. How are we going to seek justice for your dead partner if you don't help us out here?"

"Don't worry about my dead partner," Wolf said. "I take care of my own. I'll let you know if I need your help."

Sheriff Walton sat down again, his large hands gripping his knees. An odd smile creased his face. "That's why we're here, right Deputy Thomas?"

Thomas nodded.

Walton's odd smile flatlined. "You're the kind of man who takes care of things. I've known that for a long time. He elbowed the deputy. You're learning something new about your friend Mr. Wolf tonight."

Wolf yawned. "I'm glad I could educate young Deputy Thomas, but the lesson has ended. I'm going back to bed, if you'll excuse me."

Walton stood and put his hands on his hips. "There's no excuse for you. If I were you, I wouldn't plan on sleeping in your own bed tonight."

"What the hell are you talking about? Tell me what's going on?"

Walton took a step forward. "Fregiotto was shot dead in front of his beach house just twenty minutes after you left the crime scene on the beach."

"And you think I killed him?"

Deputy Thomas stood up again. "Wes, you didn't even want to take the time to look over your partner's body."

"And you didn't go over to your partner's house to let his poor wife know that he'd been killed," Walton said. "You went back to your car, took a few minutes to call your secretary and give her orders to go see Mrs. Bain, and then headed to Fregiotto's beach house to wait for him. When he arrived, you stepped out of the shadows and shot him dead. You had plenty of time to do all that."

A huge smile broke across Wolf's haggard face. He walked across the room, pivoted and faced them. Laughter erupted from deep within his chest. "So that's what this is all about! You good ol' boys kept me dangling on the side of a cliff since you got here. Now I can relax. George's death threw me a curveball, but you boys tossed a knuckler at me. Whooey! Now that I know what you're up to, things aren't so fuzzy."

"I wouldn't be so cheery if I were you," Walton said.

"Did Fregiotto die?"

"Yeah," Sheriff Walton said. "And dead men can't gripe about people who pump bullets into their hearts."

"Is that where he got it?"

Deputy Thomas nodded. "Just like your partner, but this time the shooter put four slugs in him. Wanted him deader than John Dillinger."

Wolf chuckled. "That makes things interesting." He glanced up at Sheriff Walton. "You're not ready to put the cuffs on me yet, are you?"

"I'm still seriously thinking about it."

"Let me ask a question. Was Fregiotto toting a gun?"

"He had a Glock 26 on him," Deputy Thomas said.

"Had it been fired?"

"No," Walton said.

"Did you check with the beach realtor? What did they know about him?"

"Not much," Thomas said. "He rented a four-bedroom house all by himself."

"Did you find anything on him, papers, whatever, something to tell you anything about him?"

Sheriff Walton leaned forward. "We were hoping you could do that."

Wolf spread his hands. "I've never seen the man, dead or alive."

Walton eyed him with a cold stare. "You better be telling the truth."

"Listen," Wolf drew his hands together and held them out, "if you've got enough evidence to put cuffs on me, go ahead. If not, then our little party is over."

Walton slapped at Wolf's hands, but Wolf whipped them away just in time.

Walton's hands tightened into fists. "You know me, Wolf," Walton drawled. "I'm a pitbull when it comes to finding evidence. If you killed Fregiotto, I'll put cuffs on you. You can take those words to the pawnshop and cash them in for gold."

"I believe you, Sheriff Walton," Wolf said. "Let me know if I can help."

"Keep it up, Wolf," Walton said. "You won't be such a smartass when you're wearing matching bracelets."

"You've helped us some tonight," Deputy Thomas said. "We appreciate what little you gave us."

"Yeah," Walton said, "We're begging for a full meal, and you tossed us a pea."

Wolf tilted his head. "I offered you wine with your pea, but you didn't want any."

"Shut your face!" Walton snarled and walked out the door.

"Sorry about this, Wes," Deputy Thomas said, "He's not in a good mood tonight."

"That's okay, Joel. I've never seen him in a good mood."

With a wry smile Deputy Thomas saluted and departed.

Wolf lumbered back into his bedroom, took off his clothes, crawled into bed and fell asleep.

Chapter 3

Wolf slept until ten o'clock the next morning. Before he showered, he stuck his head into the front office to see if Angie had any messages for him. She spun away from the computer screen, yawned and wagged her head no. He could tell she'd been up half the night by the circles under her eyes.

He took a long shower, ate a quick breakfast of corn flakes with a sliced banana, got dressed and sauntered back into the front office.

Angie thumbed toward his office door. "She's waiting for you in there."

"Who?"

"You know who."

"I begged you to keep her away from here."

Angie spread her hands palms up. "Who do you think I am? Your genie in a bottle? My powers are limited, and I definitely don't have the authority to issue a restraining order."

"Dammit."

Her eyes narrowed. "Listen, Mr. Boss Man, I dealt with her for three hours last night. You can spend ten minutes with her."

Wolf walked to Angie and caressed her cheek. "Sorry about that, Angel. You're a bona fide saint. She's my problem. Thanks for giving her a shoulder to cry on."

"She didn't do much crying."

Wolf took a step back and grimaced. "Yeah. She and George weren't the most faithful couple I've known."

Angie lowered her eyes and said, "You should know."

"Ouch." He rubbed his chin. "I deserved that. Listen, I'll make last night up to you. We'll go out to dinner sometime this week, my treat."

Her tired blue eyes blinked up at him. "I'll hold you to that."

His office door swung open and a striking platinum blonde peeked out. "Wes, O Wes." The woman took a deep breath and exhaled haltingly. "I need you . . . I need to talk to you."

"I'll be right in, Laura," Wolf said. He patted Angie's head, turned slowly and trudged into his office. Laura Bain closed the door behind him.

The recently widowed Mrs. Bain was outfitted in black from her wool felt hat with accompanying veil to her high-heeled shoes. She wore a sleeveless satin dress with a low V cut. She was well-endowed and proud of her endowment, always making sure the cut of her dress allowed onlookers an ample eyeful.

When he turned to face her, she rushed to him, wrapped her arms around him and buried her face in his chest. Her veiled hat fell to the floor beside them. He embraced her and patted her back. She lifted her head and planted her full lips on his. He kissed her but pulled away after a few seconds.

She buried her face on his chest again and whimpered.

"Now, now Laura," Wolf said. He rubbed her shoulders as he gazed at his partner's empty desk across the room. "I know it's hard to believe, but George is gone."

"I know," she cried. "It was a shock. I didn't think it would hit me like this."

"Well, when you live with someone for years, you can't help but feel the loss, even if you didn't get along most of the time."

She choked back her tears and coughed to gain control of herself. "We had our good times, but you know the truth. The marriage was on shaky ground. Wes . . . Wes . . . did you shoot him?"

Wolf released her shoulders and stepped away. "What?"

Her mouth fell open, and she lowered her arms. "I mean . . . I thought you might have . . . because . . . because of us . . ."

"That's a fine conclusion." Wolf drifted to his desk, sat on it and crossed his arms. "What do you mean, 'because of us'?"

She wrinkled her forehead. "You know exactly what I mean. Don't be mad at me, Wes. Not long ago we shared a passionate night. We made love to each other like two teenagers. I've never felt something so wonderful and intimate. I know you felt it too."

"Listen, Laura, it was a night to remember, but I told you the next day that we had made a mistake." He flattened his hand against the middle of his chest. "I knew in my heart that I shouldn't have crossed that line. George didn't deserve my betrayal just like he didn't deserve that bullet in his chest."

Laura walked to him and stopped a few feet away. "I know you feel guilty, but I also know you feel something more. Now there's no reason to feel guilty." She reached and grasped his hand. "I'm free. We're free. We can be together without fear or guilt or regret."

He shook his hand loose. "Didn't you just ask me if I shot your husband? What if I did? It wouldn't matter to you if I had blood on my hands?" He slapped his hand against his leg. "O Wes, we made love like two teenagers. O Wes, I know you felt it, too. Don't be so sure you know exactly how I feel because I'm not sure how I feel."

She hung her head and began to sob again.

Wolf stepped closer and put his arms around her. "Laura, Laura, I don't want to be mean to you. It's just that too much has happened in the last twenty-four hours for either of us to think clearly. Now is not the time to sort out our feelings for each other. Your husband was brutally murdered last night. You need time to deal with your loss, and I need time to figure out what I'm going to do from here."

She raised her head and blinked tears from her eyes, wet streaks glistening on her cheeks. "But you do care for me, don't you, Wes?"

"Of course, I care for you."

"I love you. I want us to be together."

"Slow down, Laura. Your heart is filled with so many emotions right now that it's hard for you to know what's real and what' not."

"I know what I feel for you is real."

"Maybe you do, but I need time."

She released him and stepped back. "Okay," she sniffled. "I don't want to crowd you. We can take our time."

"That's the best way. We'll take one day at a time and figure all this out."

He pulled a tissue from a box on his desk and handed it to her.

She wiped her eyes and cheeks. "Will you stop by and see me tonight?"

He shook his head. "It's much too soon. Be patient."

"If you say so." She bobbed her head and sniffed. "Please don't make me wait too long."

He picked her hat off the floor and handed it to her. She shifted it back and forth on her head until it was fairly level. Then he led her to the door, ushered her through the front office and said, "I'll see you soon." She placed her hand on his cheek, gave him a quick kiss on the lips and left.

Wolf headed back to his office, avoiding eye contact with Angie. He sat at his desk, clasped his hands in front of him, and stared at the wooden sign hanging on the opposite wall. It was painted with yellow words against a black background: Wolf and Bain Detective Agency.

Angie opened the door and entered. "How'd it go?"

Wolf kept his eyes on the sign. "How'd what go?"

"Did you and the widow make wedding plans?"

He shifted his focus to her. "Very funny. You're another Amy Poehler."

She walked to his desk, planted her hands on top of it and leaned toward him. "Maybe I'll head down to open mic night at Fish Heads Bar and Grill and try some one-liners."

He did a short drum roll on his desk with his fingers. "Go ahead. Break a leg." He took a deep breath and blew it out. "She thinks I murdered her husband."

"That doesn't surprise me. She believes most men would kill for her body. Now she's probably wondering when you two will tie the knot."

"Knots aren't my thing."

"I guess you were never a boy scout."

"Couldn't memorize the scout pledge. Figured life's too short."

Angie glanced at George Bain's desk. "You're right about that."

"The cops think I killed Frank Fregiotto."

"You certainly leave lethal impressions on people. Who's Frank Fregiotto?"

"The guy that George was trailing, the one Miss Couch wanted us to scare off."

She stood and put her hands on her hips. "I should have known it led back to her."

"Wasn't her fault. George knew the guy was shady. He should have been prepared."

Her eyes glossed over. "Still, Carolyn Couch didn't seem authentic to me." She blinked and refocused on Wolf. "Oh well, she's out of your life now."

Wolf set his elbows on the desk and templed his hands. "Maybe. I have a funny feeling about this mess that's been dumped into my lap."

"Are they going to charge you with anything?"

He wobbled his head. "I don't think so. They don't have much on me except flimsy circumstantial evidence."

"You're not Sheriff Walton's favorite private eye. He might conjure up something."

"That's true. I might have to solve this murder to save my own skin."

She walked around the desk and placed her hand on his shoulder. "I think you can handle Sheriff Walton. I'm not so sure about Laura Bain, though. She turns grown men into quivering teenage boys."

Wolf leaned his head against her side. "Don't worry about me. I've learned my lesson with her."

"I hope so." Her lips tightened and one eye closed. "You don't suppose she could have killed George, do you?"

Wolf laughed, withdrew his head and rocked back in his chair. "Now that's funny. Laura doesn't have the grit to kill anyone, even someone like George. Naw, I don't think she could have done it."

"You don't think so, huh? What if I told you she got to her door last night just before I arrived."

Wolf straightened. "Is that a fact?"

"Yes. I was pulling up when she was fishing for her keys on her porch. Once she entered, I gave her a few minutes before I went up and knocked."

"Hmmmm. Now where could she have been at three o' clock in the morning?"

"Were you with her last night?"

"Nooooo!"

Angie nodded slowly. "I believe you. That leaves me with one conclusion: she's a black widow."

Wolf raised a finger. "If she turns out to be the killer, I'll hire you on as my next partner."

Angie's face lit up with a boyish smile. "I'll take the job. You know I'm almost done with my online classes. I'll be certified soon."

"And I'm sure you got straight A's. Tell ya what. I'll give you two assignments to see if you have the right stuff. First, replace all the signs: the one out front, the one in your office . . ." He pointed to the opposite wall. ". . . and the one in here. I want them to say: Wolf Detective Agency. Second, I want you to do your best to keep Laura Bain away from me."

Angie frowned. "You don't have much faith in me, do you?"

Wolf knotted his brow and with a hurt tone said, "Why do you say that?"

"If you did, those signs would say: Wolf and Stallone Detective Agency."

He rubbed his hands together. "You said it yourself, Angel, you're not a genie in a bottle. Good luck with that second assignment."

The engine of Wolf's '69 Cougar rumbled as he drove slowly onto Virginia Dare Trail, the highway that hugged the coastline. He glanced to his right into Jennette's Pier parking lot. *No cop cars. Must have cleaned everything up by now.* Beach houses, surf, fishing and kite stores, and old motels with names like Owen's, Sea Foam, The Dunes, Tar Heel, Islander and Blue Heron lined the street on both sides. Beyond the buildings on the right, the dunes with their waving sea grasses blocked the view of the ocean.

Three miles farther along the road, Jockey's Ridge rose up on the left. The park boasted the tallest sand dune system in the eastern United States. The place reminded him of the Mojave Desert with little vegetation, high temperatures and burning sands. Sometimes he'd go there to take long walks in the heat of the day. He didn't mind suffering through the sweltering conditions because the surroundings gave him the sense that he had left the rotten world behind. Besides, a little suffering was good for the soul.

At the moment his soul was unsettled. Carolyn Couch's story didn't add up. Why would her friend's newfound lover kill a guy he didn't know? Even if Bain told him to get lost or else, that would be an extreme reaction. The question of who killed Fregiotto was even more puzzling. Walton's theory actually made a lot of sense. Wolf was the only one with a motive—revenging the death of his partner. Nothing else fit together. Carolyn Couch brought this muddled mess to his doorstep. She better have some answers. He remembered the name of the place she was staying—the Sandbar Bed and Breakfast. He knew the owner. For years they drank at the same bar, the Blue Crab Tavern. Wolf knew most everybody in Nags Head. He had served with the Dare County Sheriff's Department for five years before he started his own detective business. In his line of work, it paid to know people.

The Sandbar Bed and Breakfast was a three-story bright yellow beach house about a mile and a half past Jockey's Ridge along Virginia Dare Trail. The bottom two levels offered vacationers luxury accommodations and a short walk to the beach. The owner, Johnny Phelps, lived on the top level. Wolf turned left into the driveway and parked in the only open space. Three other cars, a silver Equinox, a blue CRV and crimson Ford Escape occupied the other spaces.

Wolf hustled up the outside wooden steps to the third-floor deck and rapped on the sliding glass door. The great room resembled most modern beach house layouts—cathedral ceilings and an open floor plan combining a kitchen, dining room and living room. On the far wall a bedroom door opened, and Johnny Phelps marched out dressed in a lime green t-shirt and Bermuda shorts. He recognized Wolf at once and gave him a gap-toothed grin before he slid the door open. He was a thin man, about six feet tall with slicked-down black hair parted in the middle and a thin mustache.

"Wes Wolf, how ya doing, buddy?" Phelps held out his hand. "Long time no see."

"It's been a while." Wolf shook his hand.

"Sorry to hear about your partner. I heard it on the news this morning."

"Bad news travels fast. Old George got himself into trouble last night. It'll be different without him, that's for sure. How about you? Been staying out of trouble?"

"Oh yeah. You know me. Busy, busy, busy. I plan on opening another bed and breakfast in a few weeks over on Roanoke Island. People love the Outer Banks, not that I have to tell you that."

"So business has been booming, huh?"

"Couldn't be better, in the primetime season, anyway. Now the winter is a different story. Hey, come on in and have a cup of coffee."

Wolf waved his hand. "No, no, no. I don't want to bother you. I just have a couple of questions."

"Well hell, Wes, you're no bother. What do you want to know?"

"Are you renting a room out to a couple women this week, one by the name of Emma Ritz and the other Carolyn Couch?"

Phelps tilted his head and gave a quizzical smile. "Only one of them, the Ritz girl. Never heard of anyone by the name of Carolyn Couch."

"Well maybe you just didn't catch her name. She stayed with Miss Ritz."

He shook his head. "Nope. That lady was here alone. Kept to herself, mainly. Used the pool a couple of times. Sweet looking girl, tall with short black hair and a nice body."

"No one else was with her?"

"Wait a minute. Just remembered something. A guy picked her up a few nights ago. I only got a glimpse—dark hair and sideburns. He was driving a Jeep Wrangler, dark green."

Wolf bobbed his head, picturing Miss Couch's description of Fregiotto. "I'd like to talk to her. What room did she rent?"

"She stayed in the Mermaid Room down on the first floor, but you missed her by a couple hours. She left here this morning, three days early."

Wolf brushed his knuckles along his jawline. "Did she say why?"

"Huh-uh. Just packed up her bags and left."

"What kind of car was she driving?"

"A black Mercedes. Nice car. It was one of those SLC convertibles."

"Hmmph." *Now things were totally mixed up. Who was this woman, Emma Ritz or Carolyn Couch? Whoever it was, she wanted to get out of town before anybody could ask her questions.* "Thanks, Johnny, and good luck with that new rental."

"Sure thing, Wes. We'll have to get together for a couple of beers and crab legs down at the Blue Crab one of these days."

Wolf smiled and slapped his shoulder. "Sure thing, Johnny, one of these days."

Driving back to the office, Wolf couldn't get a handle on this mysterious lady's behavior. He was definitely attracted to her. *Oh well, she left, and there's nothing I can do about it. Does it really matter? What's the next step?* Her quick departure raised too many questions. Why did she make up the story about Emma Ritz? Was she Emma Ritz? Did she have something to do with Fregiotto's death? That definitely mattered. He didn't like the idea of being the prime suspect in a murder case. Tracking her down wouldn't be easy, especially if he had to drive clear to Charlotte to find her. If she lied about her imaginary friend, she could be lying about her hometown, too.

When he entered the office, Angie glanced up from the computer screen and said, "You had a couple of visitors about twenty minutes ago."

Wolf straightened. "Let me guess: Sheriff Andy Taylor and Deputy Barney Fife?"

"Close. Sheriff Dugan Walton and that cute young deputy. What's his name?"

"Joel Thomas. What did they want?"

"They wanted to see all the guns in the office." She opened the bottom drawer of her desk to reveal a .357 Magnum revolver. "I certainly didn't want to give up my new Swiss & Wesson."

"Did they have a warrant?"

Angie shrugged. "I don't know, and I didn't ask."

"What did you tell them?"

"I told them to come back when you were here."

"That's my girl. You keep that up, and you just might be my next partner."

"Should I have my name added to the signs?"

"Not yet. Anything else happen while I was gone?"

She took a deep breath. "Yeah." Her expression seemed to chill as if the temperature had dropped twenty degrees. "Miss Couch called."

"No kidding? I wasn't expecting that. What did she say?"

"She's staying at the Comfort Inn just up the road."

"I wonder why she moved?"

Angie drummed her fingers on the desk. "I could make a good guess. She didn't come out and say it, but women's intuition tells me she wanted to be closer to you." Angie picked up a small square of paper from her desk. "Here's her room number. She wanted you to stop by."

Wolf's lips formed an impish smile. He reached, snagged the Post-it Note and waved it between them. "You probably didn't know it, Angel, but this little scrap saved me a long trip to Charlotte."

Chapter 4

The Comfort Inn South was an oceanfront hotel along Old Oregon Inlet Road about a mile north of Wolf's office. It looked like most other Comfort Inns, about seven stories high, a yellowish big block of a building with a nearly filled parking lot. Wolf squeezed the Cougar in between two SUVs at the back of the lot and cut the engine. He glanced at the scrap of paper. "Room 607," he grumbled. "Miss Carolyn Couch, you better have some answers for me."

He crossed the parking lot with long strides, passed through the lobby and headed straight for the elevators. When the doors separated, three boys carrying body boards rushed out, and Wolf barely sidestepped them. Inside the elevator he watched the digital numbers rise until the g-force diminished and the doors parted. *This should be interesting. What in the name of Aphrodite is this woman up to?*

Room 607 was halfway down the hall. He knocked, positioned himself in front of the peephole and simpered. The door opened, and the tall beauty stood there wearing a sleeveless red swing dress with a white-flower print. Her dark eyes focused on him and her red lips trembled.

"Miss Couch, I doubted I would ever see you again, but here you are, right in front of me," Wolf sneered.

She raked her fingers through her short black hair and sighed. "Please come in, Mr. Wolf."

The room had an ocean view with a king bed. Near the window a beige loveseat faced a big screen TV mounted on an off-white wall. Wolf pulled an armchair away from an oak desk and shifted it toward Miss Couch. "Shall we sit down and talk?"

She smiled a weak smile and sat down.

Wolf sat on the loveseat and leaned on his knees. "Okay, Miss Couch, where do we start?"

"I know what you're thinking," she said. "Nothing makes sense." She wrung her hands and glanced around the room. "It's all a big mess."

Wolf smirked. "That would be an underestimation of the situation."

She lowered her eyes, staring at the faux-oak laminate floor. "I'm ashamed of myself, but it was the only plan I could come up with."

Wolf waited until she made eye contact again. "Why did you need to come up with a plan?"

She took a deep breath and let it out haltingly. "I have a confession to make. My name isn't Carolyn Couch. Everything I told you yesterday was a lie."

Wolf nodded slowly. "I caught on to your . . . shall we say . . . fabrication when the dead bodies started piling up."

Trepidation filled her eyes. "It's all my fault. Mr. Bain seemed like such a nice man. Did he have a family?"

Wolf spread the fingers of each hand and touched the tips lightly. "He had a wife. No kids. Their relationship was rocky. I wouldn't feel too bad about Mr. Bain. You warned him that Fregiotto might be dangerous. He took your money without hesitation. He should have been prepared for the worst."

"I still feel awful. If I didn't walk into your office yesterday, he'd still be alive."

"Let's get back to the basics. What is your name?"

She steadied herself and looked him directly in the eyes. "Emma Ritz."

Wolf straightened, his brows rising. "That makes sense. You wanted us to scare Fregiotto away from you."

She nodded.

"Why?"

"Please be patient with me. I'm not at liberty to tell you everything."

"Then why am I here?"

"Because I need your help."

"Listen, Miss Ritz, if that is your real name." he pointed toward the door. "There's a swarm of cops, reporters and a district attorney out there waiting to pounce on me. You need to tell me everything if I'm going to work for you. Right now I'm in their sights. They think I killed Fregiotto."

She stared at the floor. "Please, Mr. Wolf, I need you to protect me from the police and the reporters." She gazed up at him. "I don't want them to know anything about me. Can you keep them from me?"

"Possibly." Wolf stood, walked to the window, and placed his hands flat against the glass. He stared at the ocean. Cumulus clouds were piling up on the horizon, and out on the sea he spotted two fishing boats seemingly on a collision course. He shook his head, turned and faced the woman. "I'd like to help you, but unless you tell me everything, I can't help you."

She placed her elbows on the armrest and buried her face in her hands. She wept, her shoulders shaking. When she looked up, her eyes were red-rimmed. "I can't tell you everything right now. I just can't. Please trust me. I'm all alone. I don't think I can handle this without you."

Wolf walked over and lay his hand gently against her cheek, using his thumb to wipe away a tear. "Are you really in that much trouble?"

She tried to nod but his hand tightened around her chin.

"How can I trust you when you've lied to me." His grip pressure increased, denting her smooth, pale skin with his fingers and thumb. "Don't you realize I know crocodile tears when I see them?"

Her eyes blazed up at him, and her face muscles tightened. He released his hand, and she said, "My tears may not be real, but I assure you I am not lying now. I can tell you *some* things but not everything."

Wolf walked back to the loveseat and sat down. "Okay, then, let's start with what happened last night."

She glanced out the window for a few seconds and then met Wolf's gaze. "I called Frank and told him I had something important to tell him that I couldn't tell him over the phone. I told him to meet me on the beach by his house at eight-thirty. I knew Mr. Bain would be watching from some secluded spot."

"George was waiting for you to pick up your imaginary friend before tailing Fregiotto."

"I know, but I didn't think that would matter. I knew Mr. Bain would follow Frank when he left the house."

Wolf nodded. "George probably figured you were late. When Fregiotto left, he went after him."

"Yes. That's what I assumed. I don't know what happened after that. I can only speculate."

"Fair enough. Give me your best guess."

She raised a thin-fingered hand and slightly scratched her cheek with those red nails. "It's dark by eight-thirty at this time of year. Mr. Bain followed him to a place on the beach where he could confront him without an audience. Once they had distanced themselves from people, he probably called out Frank's name and warned him to stay away from me. Maybe he physically threatened him. I don't know, but for some reason Frank drew his gun and shot him."

"That sounds like a reasonable reenactment." Wolf crossed his ankles and leaned back. "What kind of relationship did you have with Fregiotto?"

"He's an employee of my father. I was sent here to manage a . . . business transaction. My father figured I needed assistance, but I didn't want any help."

Wolf drew his feet in and leaned forward again. "So he was assigned to protect you?"

She shrugged. "To keep his eye on me."

"What's wrong with having someone looking out for you?"

Her eyes narrowed. "He stepped over the line. He wanted to take over the negotiations and bring in another party to complicate things."

"And you didn't want the added confusion."

"Exactly. I had everything under control. I was hoping he would back off after Mr. Bain threatened him. I wanted him to know that he could not strong arm me."

"Why didn't you call your father and have him tell Fregiotto to back off?"

"I was afraid my father might side with him."

Wolf laughed. "And that wouldn't work out in your favor."

She nodded, eyed him and bit her lower lip as if appraising his demeanor to see if she had convinced him.

"That all makes some sense. Now tell me about the business transaction."

"I can't." Her face seemed to harden like plaster.

"Then I can't help you." Wolf rose to his feet. "I can't work for someone who can't trust me enough to tell me what's going on. I hope you understand that I'm not going to take the rap for Fregiotto's murder."

"Are you going to the police?"

"I don't have to. They'll come to me. Sheriff Walton would be pleased as plum pudding to arrest me on a murder charge. Ever since I almost beat him in the last election, he's been fretting that I'll run again. When they come to my door, I'll tell them everything I know. You'll have to fend for yourself."

She hung her head. "I deserve this. I've acted like an innocent child, but I'm far from it. I've done things . . . well . . . things that good girls don't even talk about."

"We all have sinned, Miss Ritz. If you live in this world long enough, you're bound to get dirty. Don't be so hard on yourself. Anyway, it has been interesting knowing you. I hope you don't get in too much trouble." Wolf headed for the door.

"Wait!"

He froze.

"Don't leave yet."

He turned slowly and tilted his head.

"I can tell you a little about the business transaction."

Wolf put his hands on his hips. "Okay, start talking."

"A very valuable object will be transported by boat to Roanoke Island. I'm responsible for retrieving the object and selling it to a certain party who has offered a lot of money for it."

Wolf twirled his hand in front of him. "Keep going."

"That's why I moved to this hotel. Someone broke into my room at the Sandbar Bed and Breakfast. They turned the place upside down looking for the object. Fortunately, it hadn't arrived yet. That's all I can tell you."

"At least tell me what the object is."

"All I can say is that it's old, rare and valuable."

"How valuable?"

Her face appeared suddenly weatherworn; her eyes drifted into a blank stare. "So valuable that my life is at great risk throughout this entire transaction."

"I see." Wolf stepped closer. "You *are* in need of someone to watch over you."

"Yes."

"How much money do you have with you?"

"What?"

"You heard me."

"I have a little in my purse." She glanced at the leather shoulder bag sitting on the dresser.

Wolf opened it. He noticed a small revolver next to a gray wallet. He pulled out the wallet and extracted the cash that had been tucked there. He counted out twenty-two one hundred-dollar bills. "Two thousand and two hundred dollars. Do you have any more?"

"No. That's all the cash I have."

"Can you get more?"

"Uh . . . yes . . . If I need to. I've got my bank card."

"You need to. If you want me to work for you, get the money. It'll cost you five thousand dollars."

She gasped. "That seems like a lot."

Wolf pointed to his neck. "I'm sticking this way out for you. I consider my neck more valuable than any rare object on earth. Five thousand dollars is a big discount. It's up to you."

"I have no choice. I need you."

Wolf stuck the bills into the front pocket of his gaberdine pants. "I'm going to go see my lawyer and find out how much information I can withhold from the police. Perhaps I can come up with a good story to shield you from the investigators. Did they give you two key cards for this room?"

"Yes."

"Give me one."

She stood, walked to the dresser, and dug into her shoulder bag. After a few seconds of sorting through the contents, she handed him one of the key cards.

"I'll be back later this evening. I need to talk to my lawyer and find out where I stand with the Sheriff's department. Then we'll come up with a plan to keep you out from under their magnifying glass."

Her watery eyes met his. "Thank you, Mr. Wolf. I appreciate anything you can do for me."

He patted his pocket where he had stuck the bills. "Thank you, Miss Ritz, and make sure you get the rest of that money."

The law office of Jeremy J. House was located on West Saint Clair Street in Kill Devil Hills. House was the best defense attorney on the Outer Banks. Wolf trusted him. Eight years ago, he successfully defended Wolf against an excessive force charge brought against him by a drunk driver, a vacationer who resisted arrest. Not long after that Wolf resigned his position as a Dare County deputy. He and Walton had butted heads one too many times over policy and procedures. Besides, Wolf thought he could make a go of it as a private dick. Then there was that time three years ago when Walton arrested him on drunk and disorderly charges at a local karaoke bar. House got him off with twenty hours of community service. The man knew his business and welcomed Wolf's regular stops to confer with him on legal issues.

Wolf made the turn onto West St. Clair Street and pulled into one of four parking spaces in front of the law office. The building looked more like a beach house than an office. Like most other buildings on the Outer Banks, thick posts suspended the main part of the structure ten feet above the ground to protect it from storm surges. A white Chevy Cruise was parked under the left side of the building and a cobalt blue Audi Quattro under the right. The Quattro belonged to House. He loved his high-performance cars. The place wasn't fancy, a two-story abode painted pale green with white trim. Wolf hurried up the wooden steps to the first-floor deck and slipped through the office door.

"Hi, Wes," said a good-looking blonde wearing a tight-fitting gray business suit. She sat at a glass-topped desk in front of a computer screen in the brightly lit room. Her dark eyebrows made her china blue eyes beam. "Read about your partner in the morning paper. My condolences."

"Thanks, Kelly. That was a shocker."

"Is that why you're here? Are you in trouble?"

Wolf smiled. "What do you think?"

Her forehead creased. "If you are, you've come to the right place."

"Only because you keep Mr. Legal Eagle on the straight and narrow."

"You got that right."

"Hey, when are we going to go surfing?"

She eyed him suspiciously. "As soon as you learn how."

"Give me a few years and I'll be ready for those ankle busters."

"Right. By then I'll be an old maid."

"Never," Wolf protested. "You'll be a hot soccer mom with five kids."

She smiled and shook her head.

He thumbed toward a frosted glass door with House's name and *Attorney at Law* printed on it. "Is he busy?"

"Let me check." She pressed a red button on a silver console and spoke into a microphone that rose from the console like a starved cobra: "Jeremy, Wes Wolf just showed up. Do you want to see him?"

"No!" came the harsh reply.

She nodded toward the door. "Go right in."

House was a fit man, just under six feet tall. For a guy in his late forties, he still had a thick head of brown curly hair. He always wore a crimson tie with a white dress shirt which contrasted with his olive skin. If he tried, he could grow a thick beard in three days. His five o'clock shadow usually arrived by two in the afternoon.

Wolf plopped down in the padded armchair across from his desk, took a deep breath and blew it out. "You're not going to believe this."

House removed his blue-framed reading glasses and flipped them onto the desk. "Don't tell me. Sheriff Dugan Walton caught you pissing off Jeanette's Pier and slapped you with a $500 fine."

"I wish."

"Worse?"

"Much worse."

House leaned forward, his hands on the armrests of his leather swivel chair. "You don't look that rattled to me."

"I'm not."

"Then what's the problem?"

"Murder."

"Your partner's murder?"

"No. The guy that killed him."

House leveled his pointer finger at him. "You're a suspect? Walton thinks you wanted revenge?"

"That's right, but I'm not too worried about it."

"Dammit to hell, Wes. A well-respected lawman wants to put a murder rap on you, and you're not concerned?"

"Maybe a little, but there's something else. You see, I've got this client who's in trouble."

House clasped his hands in front of him on the desk. "The house is on fire, but you're worried about watering the flowers."

"What?"

"Never mind. Tell me about your client."

"She and the guy that was killed, Frank Fregiotto, were working together."

"Did she have something to do with his murder?"

"No, but she is genuinely concerned about being dragged into this investigation. They know she's out there, but they don't know who she is."

"Okay." He took a pen from his breast pocket and tapped it a few times on the desk. "Why doesn't she want to get involved?"

"Let's just say she is on an important assignment, a once in a lifetime opportunity, and any kind of public notoriety would blow her boat out of the water."

"And she wants you to insulate her from the investigation."

"Exactly, but I'm not sure if I can legally claim client privileges under these circumstances. I'm not a lawyer or a priest. Can they make me give up information that would put her in the spotlight?"

"If this was a court trial they could certainly put you under oath, but it's not. Of course, they could claim obstruction of justice, but that's a high tight rope to walk under these circumstances."

Wolf grinned. "So legally, I can keep my mouth shut?"

House spread his hands. "Why the hell not? You've done much worse. Until they put you under oath go ahead and claim your client's privilege. If they put the hammer down on you, let them know that I've got your back."

Wolf stood and extended his hand. "You're a helluva good buddy, Jeremy."

House shook his hand. "And you're a sonovabitch."

"Ha ha! You got that right."

Late that afternoon Wolf sat in his office, hands clasped behind his head, leaning back in his swivel chair, thinking about Emma Ritz. She was starting to get to him. His last romantic tryst was with Laura Bain. Big mistake. Why was he so attracted to troubled women? Or was it women who could cause him trouble? Common sense told him he shouldn't go down that road with a gal who could sell a timeshare to a conman. Regrettably, he didn't always listen to common sense. Another part of his body commanded his attention. He pressed the button on the intercom and said, "Angel, could you step in here for a few minutes. I need your opinion about something."

Angie entered his office wearing beige pleated pants and a black, sleeveless top. To Wolf, she was an attractive girl with a tomboy temperament. Seduction was not a part of her mode of operation. With Angie what you saw was what you got. He couldn't have asked for a better secretary.

"What's up, Mr. Boss Man?" she said.

"What do you think about Emma Ritz?"

Her smile deflated. "To be honest, I'm not too impressed."

"Why not?"

"She's disingenuous."

Wolf clasped his hands and twiddled his thumbs. "I can see your point. She lies. She gave us a fake name. She's involved in some kind of mysterious underhanded business deal. But other than that, don't you think she's an okay gal?"

Angie snorted. "You are hopeless. What's in your DNA that makes you fall for these kinds of women?"

Wolf raised a hand. "Okay, okay, I get your gist, but don't sell me short. I haven't fallen for her yet."

"I see it written all over your face. If you have a fatal flaw, that's it—unscrupulous females."

He waved at her. "Ah c'mon. I'm not that bad."

"You need to be careful, Wes. If I had to deal with her, I'd be extremely cautious."

"Don't worry about me, Angel. Me and the Tin Man have no worries when it comes to falling in love." He pounded his chest. "Did you hear the echo?"

The sound of the outer office door opening and closing caught their attention.

"No," Angie said, "but I did hear someone just come in."

Wolf pointed toward the outer office. "Better go see who."

A minute passed as Wolf watched two blurry figures through the frosted glass. Then Angie swung open his office door. "Detective Wolf, this is Hugh Underdonk. He would like to speak to you."

"Come right in, Mr. Underdonk." Wolf motioned to one of the armchairs facing his desk. "Have a seat."

Underdonk was a short man, less than five feet four inches tall. He reminded Wolf of a penguin, the way he walked and dressed. He had a large round head, bald on top with black stringy long hair on the sides. He wore an indigo-violet Brooks Brothers suit with a matching bowtie against a white silk dress shirt. A thin black mustache lined his upper lip below a pug nose. Two rings sparkled on his delicate right hand, one set with a large diamond and the other an oval of jade. When he sat down, he crossed his right leg over his left knee like a woman sits when wearing a dress.

"Good afternoon, Mr. Wolf. Thank you for seeing me." His voice sounded southern, nasally and squishy as if his suit were compacting his lungs too tightly.

"Not a problem, Mr. Underdonk." Wolf beamed an ingratiating smile. "That's why I'm in business. Now, what can I do for you?"

He raised the pointer finger of his left hand. "First may I offer my heartfelt solace concerning the recent death of your partner. I read about it in this morning's paper."

"Certainly, I appreciate your kind words, but life goes on."

"Yes, it truly does. Forgive me for bringing up such morbid matters, but the paper mentioned a second murder, one involving a man named Fregiotto. Would you happen to know anything about his death?"

Wolf scooted closer to his desk. "I might. Why do you ask?"

"He was an . . . acquaintance of mine. I thought perhaps your partner's death and his were related." Underdonk fingered the jade stone on his right hand. "Fregiotto had recently contacted me about an item that I was interested in purchasing."

"Was it an old and valuable item?"

Underdonk eyed him coolly. "Yes, quite old and quite valuable."

"Ahh . . . go on, Mr. Underdonk. I find this conversation *quite* interesting."

"He was working with a woman by the name of Dare."

Wolf rubbed his chin. "That doesn't ring a bell."

"Virginia Dare."

"Now that rings a bell, sir." He pointed toward the door. "The highway that runs along the ocean about a mile from here is called Virginia Dare Trail. Was she named after the road?"

"You've got . . . *quite* . . . the sense of humor, Mr. Wolf. Of course, the highway was named after her in a roundabout way."

"Of course." Wolf had no idea what the pint-sized man was talking about except for the revelation that Emma Ritz had a new alias. "Perhaps I know this Virginia Dare by another name."

"Emma Ritz?"

"Yes."

"Did she hire you to help her secure this old and valuable item?"

Wolf raised his hands in protest. "Now, Mr. Underdonk, certainly you don't expect me to divulge confidential information between me and a client. That wouldn't be ethical."

His eyes grew narrow. "How much is she paying you?"

Wolf raised his eyebrows. "Do you think I can be bought?"

"I'll double it."

Wolf shook his head no.

"Triple it."

Wolf straightened. "Are you serious? That would be twenty thousand dollars."

"Deadly serious. But first I want to search your office to make sure the Dare Diary isn't here."

Wolf chuckled. "I would never let you do that. I consider my office my sanctuary."

Underdonk reached into his suit jacket, pulled out a small handgun and pointed it at Wolf's chest. He stood. "I'm sorry, Mr. Wolf, but I must search your office before I can work out a deal with you for that much money."

As Wolf slowly raised his hands, he managed to hit the button on the intercom. "I don't take kindly to someone aiming a gun at me in my own office, Mr. Underdonk."

"I apologize, but I must be sure the diary isn't here before I fork over twenty thousand dollars."

"So you intend to steal it from me if it's here?"

Underdonk's upper lip curled. "Not really. It doesn't belong to you, or Miss Dare or her father Thomas Ellis. It belongs to the one who possesses it. I intend to possess it if it's here."

"Put down the gun, Mr. Underdonk," Angie Stallone commanded. She stood in the doorway, holding a .357 Magnum revolver with both hands.

Underdonk glanced over his shoulder.

Wolf grinned. "I'd listen to her if I were you. Hers is much bigger than yours."

Chapter 5

Underdonk's eyes watered as he lowered the gun onto the desk. He blinked to keep tears from escaping.

"That's a good boy," Wolf said. "Now put your hands up."

He raised his hands, his lips trembling.

"Keep that gun on him, Angel, while I check his pockets." Wolf picked up Underdonk's small handgun, a Beretta Nano, from the desk and stuck it in his pants pocket.

"You fools," Underdonk blubbered. "I would have paid you the money to get the diary for me."

Wolf checked the man's back pockets and retrieved a brown leather wallet. He lofted it onto the desk. The other back pocket was empty. "Make up your mind, Underdonk. Do you want to rob me or pay me?" He funneled his hand into Underdonk's right front pocket and found a set of car keys for a Jaguar.

His voice trembled as he said, "Certainly, you understand my position. Why should I pay you for something that is not yours?"

"You don't make much sense." Wolf circled him and checked his jacket pockets.

"If I can't take it from you, that's when I'll pay you to get it for me."

"I hope you're convinced," Wolf waved toward Angie. "She's my guardian angel. She doesn't like it when people try to take things from me."

Wolf went through the rest of his pockets one by one, tossing the contents onto the desk. Then he circled back around the desk and sat in his chair. "Have a seat Mr. Underdonk, and let's see what we got here. Angel, you can put the gun down and relax."

Underdonk wiped his eyes with his dainty fingers and lowered himself onto the seat.

Angie slid the other chair several feet away from Underdonk and sat down, laying the Smith & Wesson across her lap. "Don't do anything stupid," she said. "I'm the top student in my firearms class."

"Congratulations." He glanced at her with anxious eyes. "Most secretaries excel in typing."

Wolf extracted a bunch of bills from the wallet and counted out the money. "Two thousand and seven hundred dollars, all Benjamins. Not too shabby." He looked over the other items—a passport, checkbook, several credit cards, a driver's license, a few business cards, cellphone, a box of breath mints, a lavender silk handkerchief, car keys and a ticket for *The Lost Colony* outdoor drama. "You are rolling in it, aren't you Mr. Underdonk? A nice car, lots of cash, an expensive suit."

"I wouldn't be here to purchase the diary if I wasn't well supplied."

"Let's talk about that diary. How much are you willing to pay for it?"

"I'll pay what you asked—twenty thousand dollars."

"How much were you offering Fregiotto?"

"About that much."

"But he had to pay his boss, Thomas Ellis, wasn't that his name? And then there's daughter Virginia and her commission. That would be a lot more than twenty grand, wouldn't it?"

He fingered his jade ring. "I'm a serious buyer. I'm willing to work out a deal."

"But you weren't the original buyer, were you?"

"No. Fregiotto contacted me. There's nothing wrong with a little competition to boost the bidding."

"Except . . . " Wolf raised a finger . . . "now Fregiotto is dead."

"That is true."

"I'm assuming your competition whacked him."

"That would be my guess."

"Doesn't that frighten you? Wasn't he killed in order to scare you off?"

"I'm not sure why he was killed," Underdonk wheezed. "Perhaps he got into an argument with the wrong person . . ." he took another breath . . ." someone who was faster on the draw."

"Maybe someone tried to convince him to send you away, but he refused."

"Perhaps."

Wolf spread his hands. "What if I produced the diary right now, right here, right before your eyes. Forget about Thomas Ellis and daughter Virginia. How much would you give me for it?"

"A hundred thousand dollars. I'd write you out a check immediately."

Wolf ran his knuckles along his jaw line. "That must be some diary." He glanced at Angie, "Angel, have you ever heard of the Dare Diary?"

Angie shrugged. "Never heard of it."

Underdonk grasped the edge of the desk and leaned against it, his eyes bulging. "Do you have it?"

"No."

He sat back. "I didn't think so."

"But I will. Emma Ritz, I mean Virginia Dare hired me to get it. She will inform me when it's coming and where to pick it up."

Underdonk frowned. "But she and I have had troubles in the past. She won't sell it to me."

"She's working with me now. I can't guarantee that she will sell it to you, but I can guarantee you a meeting with her. You'll be given a chance to plead your case."

Underdonk sat quietly for a minute. His lower lip protruded, and his eyes stared at the scattered items on the table. "I guess I have no other choice. When will we meet?"

Wolf picked up one of Underdonk's business cards from the pile of items on the desk and read it: "Hugh Underdonk – Antiquities Dealer, Lafayette, Louisiana. Is this your cell phone number?"

"Yes," he hissed.

"Where are you staying?"

"At the Burrus House Inn on Roanoke Island."

"I'll call you tomorrow and let you know."

Underdonk spread his hands. "May I gather my belongings?"

Wolf picked up the stack of cash. "Everything but this."

The small man's mouth fell open. "You intend to rob *me*?"

"No, no, of course not." He lifted the bills and thumbed them like a deck of cards. "Two thousand seven hundred dollars—that's my fee for setting up the meeting. Do we have a deal?"

Underdonk closed his eyes and nodded slowly. "I feel like I'm making a deal with Mephistopheles." He opened his eyes and gazed at Wolf like a sad hound dog. "May I have my gun back. I don't feel safe without it."

"I don't blame you," Wolf howled. "Sure. Sure. I wouldn't want to lose a potential buyer because he was unarmed." Wolf raised a finger. "But don't be like my partner. He got shot in the chest with his rod still in his pocket."

"Don't worry. I intend to be vigilant." Underdonk leaned and picked the items from the desk, sticking them one by one back into his pockets.

Wolf stood and fished the Beretta Nano out of his pants pocket. He walked around his desk as Underdonk rose to his feet and placed the gun in his soft outstretched hand.

Underdonk raised the gun and pointed it at Wolf. "I should shoot you for humiliating me."

Wolf leaned his head toward Angie. With both hands she held the Smith & Wesson revolver aimed at his chest.

Underdonk smiled sheepishly. "I was just kidding, of course."

"I'm not," Angie said. "Put your gun away."

Underdonk slipped it into his jacket pocket.

Wolf grinned. "Like I said before, hers is much bigger than yours." He gripped Underdonk's shoulders, turned him around and directed him out the front door.

When Wolf reentered his office, Angie was still sitting on the wooden armchair, inspecting her firearm. She glanced up, held the pistol so that the end of the barrel was just below her lips and blew.

"You are truly my guardian angel."

"Do you really believe that?"

"Sure."

Angie slid the gun onto the top of the desk. "Then let's put my name on those signs."

Wolf's eyes lit with merriment. "I'm seriously thinking about it."

An earnest expression formed on her boyish face. "One more semester and I'll be done with my online law enforcement certification."

"I'll add that to your résumé." Wolf opened a cabinet to the left of the doorway and lifted out a bottle of red wine and two glasses. "It's been a stressful day. What's say we take the edge off with some Napa Valley Red." He filled the wine glasses to the brim and handed one to Angie.

She leaned back and took a sip. "Ahhhh, that's good."

"What did you think of our oddball client?"

"You played along with him like you'd seen his act before."

"That's because there's money to be made here. Lots of it."

She took another sip of wine. "More importantly, there's a murder to be solved, one that would remove the noose from your neck."

"Thanks for reminding me." Wolf rubbed his neck and grinned. "I did learn a few new things from our powwow with Mr. Underdonk."

"For instance?"

"The new name of Miss Ritz. What do you know about Virginia Dare?"

"Your client or the historical figure?"

"The historical figure."

"The basics that most people around here know. She was the first English baby born in America." She pointed toward the open office door. "Her mother gave birth to her just a few miles from here on Roanoke Island back in the late 1500's. Queen Elizabeth hoped to establish a permanent English colony, but they didn't last long."

"Right." Wolf rubbed his chin. "They disappeared, vanished in thin air and became America's greatest mystery."

Angie leaned forward, elbows on her knees, wine glass tilted slightly in her right hand. "There are a lot of theories about what happened to them, but no one really knows."

"Do you find it interesting that Underdonk said Virginia Dare Trail was named after my client in a roundabout way?"

"That is fascinating. He must believe that she's a direct descendant."

"Right, and her parents named her after that long-lost ancestor."

"That would be highly unlikely," Angie said.

"Why?"

"If they all died on that island, how could there be any direct descendants?"

"Good point, but then there's this Dare Diary."

"Yeah." She took a big gulp of wine and wiped her lips with her hand. "We don't know much about it. Who wrote it? What's in it? How much is it worth? Who owns it?"

"We know it's old and valuable."

Angie raised her eyebrows. "So valuable that people are willing to commit murder to get their grubby hands on it."

Wolf finished off his wine and set the glass on the desk. "I think I'll head over to the bookstore in Manteo tomorrow morning and pick up a book on the Lost Colony."

"That's a shocker."

"What do you mean?"

"When's the last time you bought a book?"

"I can't even remember the last time I read a book."

Chapter 6

After Angie left the office, Wolf poured himself another tall glass of wine. He wished he would have paid more attention in history class. He had never gone to see *The Lost Colony* play at the outdoor theater on Roanoke Island, only a few miles from where he lived. He remembered seeing a ticket for the drama when he emptied Underdonk's pockets. It was dated for that evening's 7:45 show. *I need to go see that play one of these days. Maybe I'll take Angie. No time now. Hopefully, I can find a book that will catch me up on the backstory.*

At seven o'clock he decided to go see Virginia Dare. He figured she was anxious to hear about his visit with his lawyer, Jeremy House. Now he had some leverage. *Yes, indeed, there's money to be made here.* He headed out the door and climbed into his '69 Cougar. He turned the key, and the engine roared to life. The rumble of the idling car energized him. The last two days had been draining, but he felt ready to go.

At the corner of East Hunter Street and Old Oregon Inlet Road he noticed a silver Buick Cascada parked off to the side. *That's odd.* A young guy wearing a brown Gatsby cap and shades sat at the wheel. Wolf turned north and headed in the direction of the Comfort Inn. A few hundred yards down the road, he glanced into his rearview mirror and noticed the Cascada trailing him. About a mile up the road he turned into the Comfort Inn parking lot and found a parking space in front near the lobby. After stepping out of the car and closing the door, he peered over his shoulder to see the Cascada back into a space at the back of the lot. Wolf laughed and shook his head. *I'm becoming a very popular private eye.*

He walked leisurely through the hotel lobby to the elevators. *This should be an interesting conversation.* Standing in the elevator, watching the digital number rise, he imagined kissing and fondling Emma Ritz. He shook the fantasy from his mind. *Carolyn Couch, Emma Ritz, Virginia Dare — which is it? Get control of your raging testosterone levels, you satyr.* He took a deep breath and tried to relax. The doors parted, and he strode down the hall to her room, slipped the key card out of his front pants pocket, waved it in front of the sensor, and when the green light flashed, he opened the door.

Virginia Dare gasped and then said, "Oh, it's you." She was sitting on the loveseat with a thick romance novel in her hands.

"Who were you expecting, the pizza delivery boy?"

Color flooded her pale face, and she smiled. "I've been thinking about you." She dropped the paperback onto the loveseat.

"Uh huh. Good thoughts, I hope."

Her smile flashed a hint of seduction. "*Very* good."

"*Very* good is good. I've got *very* good news for you."

She quickly stood and stepped toward him, eyes widening. "Did you talk to your lawyer?"

"Oh yeah. We had a *very* good talk."

"And . . . "

"If I decide to take your case, I can claim client privilege as far as your identity is concerned. That is as long as they don't call me into court and put me under oath."

She took a deep breath and exhaled. "That's wonderful! You will help me, won't you? You said you would. I paid you."

"You paid me about half. Did you get the rest of the money?'

"Yes. It's in my shoulder bag."

Wolf ran his knuckles along his jawline, feeling the prickle of his four-day beard. "I don't know. I ran into a friend of yours and discovered that you've been lying to me again."

Her jaw dropped, and her eyes widened. "What friend?"

"He said his name is Hugh Underdonk."

"He's no friend of mine!" Her eyes flamed. "Where did you see him?'

"In my office."

She crossed her arms and tucked in her chin. "You're not going to listen to him, are you?"

"I don't know. He offered me a lot of money for a certain old and valuable object. I told him I could get it for him."

"How dare you!"

"How dare I what, Miss Dare?"

A small gasp escaped her mouth.

"That's right. He also told me your new name—Virginia Dare."

She frowned. "It's not a new name. It's my real name."

"It has a familiar ring in these parts."

"What else did he tell you?"

"He told me what the object was."

The color drained from her face. She hung her head, trudged to the loveseat and collapsed on it.

"Are you all right?"

Her eyes peered up under thick black lashes. "I don't know. Everything is falling apart. I can't believe you're siding with Hugh Underdonk. You had no right to tell him you could get your hands on the diary." She pointed at her chest. "I'm the one who knows when and where it will arrive. I'm the one who's authorized to pick it up and make the transaction."

Wolf stood over her and placed his hands on his hips. "Listen to you. My neck's in the noose. You lassoed me into this mess. I don't take risks without the opportunity to reap rewards. Either you trust me to handle the diary, or I'm cutting bait and going home."

"You don't understand." She buried her face in her hands.

"What don't I understand?"

She lifted her head and glared at him. "I hate Hugh Underdonk. I can't stand him. I refuse to do business with him."

"Okay then, you're on your own." Wolf walked halfway across the room, skidded to a stop and turned. "I thought the news from my lawyer would make you happy, but you're impossible. You don't have to like someone to do business with him. Anyway, I quit." He turned to go.

"Wait!" She stood and rushed to him. "Please don't tell the investigators about me."

"I have to. You are no longer my client. I'll be charged with obstruction."

She began to swoon, and Wolf clasped her shoulders. She steadied herself and gazed up at him. He gripped the back of her head and kissed her, a long, hard kiss.

When their lips parted, she caught her breath and swallowed. "You do care for me," she said.

"I want to help you, but you're being impossible."

"Trust me, Wes, when I tell you that Underdonk is pure evil."

"Why?"

"I can't talk about that right now. Just trust me."

"If I'm going to trust you, then you need to trust me."

"I do trust you."

Wolf patted himself on the chest. "Then let me pick up the diary and deliver it."

She inhaled slowly and nodded. "Okay. Maybe it's better that way."

"Sure it is. I know how to handle myself. You would be at much greater risk. Obviously, people are willing to kill for a chance to possess it."

She exhaled and her body seemed to deflate against him like a punctured blowup kid's toy. "But I . . . I abhor the thought of dealing with Underdonk. He's the last person to whom I'd want to sell the diary."

"Don't worry about Underdonk. I just want to make some money off him."

She raised her head. "What do you mean?"

"I'm stringing him along and taking his money while I do it. We don't have to sell the diary to him."

"He's going to give you money?"

"He already has." Wolf sneered and winked. "I only guaranteed him one thing."

"What's that?"

"A meeting with you."

She clasped her hands against her ears. "No, no, no. I can't stand to be in the same room with him."

"Don't worry, Darling. I'll be there. We'll talk, and it will be over in fifteen minutes. He'll leave believing he has a chance to bid on the diary. I'd never let him hurt you."

Her eyes iced over. "I'm not worried about him harming me. I'm worried about me killing him. When is this meeting?"

"Tomorrow evening at my place. When does the diary arrive?"

She hesitated, her lips losing their fullness as she pressed them tightly together. Finally, she said, "On Saturday afternoon."

"That's perfect. We've got two days to set this up. Now tell me about the Dare Diary."

"There's not much to tell."

"C'mon. Who wrote it? Why is it so valuable? What's in it?"

She drifted across the room to the window and stared at the ocean. "You've heard of the Lost Colony?"

"Of course."

"One of the colonists, a woman by the name of Eleanor Dare, kept a diary. It explains the disappearance of the lost colony."

"It survived all these years?"

She nodded. "Her father, John White, was an artist. They took plenty of paper and ink with them. She kept it for all those years. It even has little drawings and maps in it. Believe me, the diary tells the whole story."

"Whadaya know. I guess it would be worth a lot of money."

Virginia appraised him dubiously. "Do you always come up with such astute deductions?"

Wolf flashed a schoolboy smile. "Most of the time. By the way, didn't your parents name you after Eleanor's daughter."

"Yes, her daughter Virginia. I'm a direct descendant of Eleanor."

"Ah . . ." he raised a finger . . . "That's easy to say because your last name is Dare, but can you prove it?"

She walked to the dresser, opened her shoulder bag and extracted a folded piece of paper. She pivoted and held it up. "Check this out."

He crossed the room, took the paper and unfolded it. "What's this?"

"A DNA test."

"This says, 'Test Subject – Virginia Eleanor Ellis.'"

"That's my name, but I go by Virginia Dare. The DNA test traced my line of DNA's paternal strands back to Thomas Ellis, one of the original colonists. He married the widow Eleanor Dare. Her husband and daughter had been killed by local natives. It's all in the diary."

"This case is becoming more and more fascinating." He handed Virginia the DNA analysis. "While you're putting that back into your purse, could you retrieve the balance of the money you owe me?"

She glowered at him but found her wallet and fished out the remaining two thousand six hundred dollars. "There's no discount for a stolen kiss?"

"Discount?" Wolf snickered. "You're lucky I don't charge you extra. My kisses don't come cheap."

Her eyes narrowed to a thin dark sliver. "Mine either." She handed him the money.

He tucked the bills into his pants pocket and then touched his forefinger to her full lips. "Fair enough. We'll skip the kiss goodnight for financial reasons, but before I leave, I need to ask a question. Do you know a young guy who wears a brown Gatsby cap and drives a silver Buick Cascada?"

"No, why?"

"He tailed me here."

"Maybe he works for Underdonk."

"I'm going to find out."

"What if he's after me?"

"Don't worry. It's my job to protect you."

Wolf stepped to the door and opened it. Virginia followed him. "No need to see me out," he said.

She grabbed the collar of his Polo shirt, pulled him down and kissed him hungrily. After what seemed like more than a minute their lips broke apart, and she stepped back.

"Whooey!" He held out his hand. "That'll be another hundred dollars."

She laughed, twirled him around and shoved him out the door.

As Wolf passed through the Comfort Inn lobby, he checked his watch: 9:20. He still had time to drive over to Roanoke Island and catch Underdonk when the play let out. Striding to his car, he noticed the night was comfortably warmer compared to the night before. A gentle breeze tousled his unruly hair. As he inserted his key to unlock the car door, he checked to see if Gatsby Boy still waited at the back of the parking lot. *Yep. Still there. Hopefully, he'll follow me.*

He slid into the car, started the engine, backed out and headed toward the exit. Turning right, he drove slowly out of the parking lot and headed north along Old Oregon Inlet Road. He puttered along at about fifteen mph, waiting to see if the Cascada trailed him. If not, he'd have to turn back and make sure the thug didn't entertain malicious intensions toward Virginia. He clicked on his left turn signal and slowed, glancing into the rearview mirror. *There he is, right on cue. Okay, Gatsby Boy, follow me over to Roanoke Island.* He turned left onto Gulfstream Street, drove a block to the stop sign and checked the mirror. *Yep, still there.* He hit the accelerator and headed west onto Route 12 which joined with Route 64 and crossed the Washington Baum Bridge to Roanoke Island. Wolf applied more pressure to the accelerator and took the Cougar up to fifty mph. The Cascada kept its distance but kept pace.

The town of Manteo was named after some friendly Native American; at least Wolf knew that much about the local history. It was a quaint old town, its streets lined with modest homes, souvenir shops, traditional stores, good restaurants, fast food chains and gas stations. The big draw of the place was Roanoke Island Festival Park along Shallowbag Bay. Here families could go to experience how the early settlers and Native Americans lived back in the late 1500s. Wolf had walked through the park a few times and found the interactive exhibits interesting.

The outdoor venue for *The Lost Colony* play, however, was located on the northwest side of the Island near the Elizabethan Gardens and old historic Fort Raleigh. After driving several miles along Route 64, Wolf turned onto Fort Raleigh Road, which was shrouded by tall trees and thick woods. At this time of night the trees loomed like giants, their boughs waving in the breeze against the starlit sky. He checked the rearview mirror and caught a glimpse of the Cascada's headlights about two hundred yards behind him.

The back of the parking lot offered a few open spaces. Wolf drove to the far end and slotted into a spot between a Volkswagen Beetle and a Chevy Tahoe. He got out and stood, eyeing the entrance of the lot. The Cascada entered and pulled into one of the first empty spaces. *Now to find the Jaguar.* He assumed Underdonk arrived early. He seemed like a man who valued control over his circumstances, a finicky type easily agitated when things go wrong. Wolf headed to the front of the lot and located the Jaguar near the entrance. *Hopefully, there's not more than one Jaguar in this lot.* He checked his watch—9:40. *Perfect timing.* He leaned against the driver's side window and crossed his arms. A big flood light on a pole nearby lit the car, an F-Type model, and Wolf noticed its deep violet color. Wolf chuckled to himself, remembering Underdonk's suit and lavender silk handkerchief. *The guy likes the color purple.*

A few minutes later the outdoor theater goers spilled into the parking lot. Underdonk was one of the first ones to get to his car. He stopped abruptly when he saw Wolf and inserted his hand into his jacket pocket. "W-What do you want?" Underdonk sputtered.

Wolf held out his hands. "Take it easy. I'm working for you, remember?"

Underdonk glanced around anxiously, checking to see if anyone was near enough to hear them. "You said you were going to call me to set up the meeting," he whispered harshly.

"Face to face is much more personal, don't you think?"

"No," he continued in his low tone. "Not in a dark parking lot without any kind of warning. You're lucky I didn't shoot you."

Wolf directed his gaze to the back corner of the parking lot where Gatsby Boy had parked. "You're a jumpy little monkey, but maybe you have reason to be."

"What are you talking about?"

"Do you have a young guy working for you, maybe twenty-one or twenty-two years old, wears a Gatsby cap and drives a silver Buick Cascada?"

Underdonk's eyes grew wide. "No." He stuck his hand back into his jacket pocket, raised his head and tried to see above the cars in the direction Wolf was staring. "Are you being followed?"

"The guy's been tailing me all night."

"He is not under my employ."

"I wanted to make sure because I might have to put an ass-thumpin' on him."

"Be my guest and give him a swift kick in the balls for me."

Wolf chuckled and eyed Underdonk. "Maybe I will. I wonder who he is."

"I'd bet all the money I gave you yesterday that he's Bacon's gunman."

"Who's Bacon?"

"Alfred Bacon, another antiquities dealer. He's my competition."

"Ahhhhh, I see. No wonder you're so damn jumpy. The guy is following me to find you."

"That's possible." Underdonk stepped to the Jaguar and leaned against it, slightly shielded by Wolf. "Do you have a gun on you?"

"Of course."

"What are we going to do?"

"Wait."

"For what?"

"For the parking lot to empty out. I have a feeling he'll leave with the crowd. He doesn't want to be too obvious. We'd be safer inside your car just in case he has lethal objectives."

Underdonk fished for his keys and hurriedly jabbed the remote button, and the locks released. He threw open the door and scrambled behind the wheel. Wolf strolled around the car, opened the door and eased into the front passenger's side. Randomly, around the parking lot car engines started, and headlights beamed on. Within fifteen minutes the lot emptied. The silver Cascada was gone.

"Do you want me to follow you back to your hotel?" Wolf asked.

"No." Underdonk slipped his gun out of his pocket and placed it in the cupholder between the seats. "You lead the way out of here. I'll stay back at a good distance. If you see him, hit your brake twice to warn me."

"Sounds like a plan. You don't seem so worried about him now."

Underdonk pulled his silk handkerchief from his front breast pocket and wiped his forehead. "I've had time to think about it. I don't believe Bacon has made the connection between me and you yet."

"Maybe not. Why do you think he's following me?"

"For the same reason I stopped by your office yesterday. Bacon is a highly intelligent man. He read about the two murders in the newspaper this morning and linked your detective agency to Virginia Dare. He's keeping tabs on you because he wants the diary."

"That's a very insightful conclusion," Wolf said. "I agree with you." Wolf lifted the handle, shoved the door open, and the interior light flashed on. It reflected off the top of Underdonk's bald head, creating deep shadows under his brow and cheeks. His stringy hair that rimmed the sides and the severe lighting made him look like a late-night horror show host. "By the way, We're meeting with Virginia Dare tomorrow evening at eight o'clock in my office."

"I'll be there. Tell her to be kind to me."

"Don't get your hopes up."

Wolf stepped out of the car, slung the door shut and headed to his Cougar. On the drive home he didn't see the silver Cascada. He busied his mind with all the possibilities of the circumstances that had unraveled before him these last two days. More than anything, he wanted to set up a meeting with Alfred Bacon. *If I play my cards right, there could be quite a windfall. Yes, indeed! There's money to be made here.*

Chapter 7

At ten 'o clock the next morning Wolf drove back across the Washington Baum Bridge to Manteo. Gatsby Boy wasn't parked along the side of the road this time, watching for him. Wolf figured his boss had other dirty deeds that needed done. Sooner or later, though, he knew that he and Gatsby Boy were going to rock and roll.

Downtown Books was located on Sir Walter Raleigh Street near the Roanoke Island Festival Park. Wolf didn't spend much time in bookstores. When he did read, he preferred nonfiction. He knew he needed to acquire some background information on the Lost Colony. Hopefully, he could find a good book to enlighten him, preferably one with less than two hundred pages. The DNA results Virginia Dare had showed him seemed legit, despite her poor track record of telling the truth. Was it even likely that a direct descendant could be traced to Eleanor Dare? He needed to keep an open mind and explore the documented history to determine what was possible. Besides, he figured he'd have more success dealing with Underonk and Bacon if he knew what he was talking about.

Wolf parked across the street from the bookstore, a well-kept redbrick building with large mullioned windows that welcomed sunshine into the front of the shop. Four dormers fronted a barn-style roof, and on the right side of the structure white steps led up to a second and third story deck. As he crossed the street, the courthouse bell bonged like an oversized Chinese gong. *Must be ten o'clock.* Wolf checked his watch. *Yep.* He neared the entrance and noticed a sign in one of the window squares that read: *When something goes wrong in your life, just yell, "Plot Twist!" and move on.* Wolf chuckled. *Sounds like my last two days.*

He entered the store and caught a whiff of lemon incense. Two brass chandeliers hung on each side of the entryway. *I should be able to see the light in this place.* He drifted around the aisles and shelves, not exactly sure where to go. He noticed a small blondish dog, some kind of terrier, stretched out on pillow at the back of the store. He headed in that direction and stopped halfway there at a large black table displaying a variety of local titles: wild horses, nature photography, books about lighthouses, fishing, and shipwrecks. A sharp looking brunette with blonde highlights approached him. She wore large hooped earrings and a colorful beaded necklace that contrasted against her pine green tank top. She had a natural look about her, a slight tan and freckles on her shoulders.

A warm smile brightened her oval face. "Good morning. You look like you need some help."

"Yes," Wolf said, feeling like a Baptist preacher in a liquor store. He glanced around the room. "I'm looking for the local history section."

She hooked her finger toward her. "Follow me."

"Is that your guard dog back there?"

She laughed. "That's Piper. He might lick you to death."

He trailed her toward the front of the store where she made a right and headed to the far wall. She stopped in front of a large bookshelf. A sign on top touted: *Check out our local history books!* "Perfect," Wolf said.

She winked. "If you need any more help, let me know."

She turned to go, and Wolf said, "Hold on there. I could use some professional help."

She about-faced. "Okay. I'm a professional, at least when it comes to buying and selling books."

"Do you have any good books on the Lost Colony?"

She laughed and waved toward the books. "That top shelf is full of them."

"Which one do you recommend?"

She reached and pulled down a thick tome entitled *The Mystery of the Lost Colony*. "This one is very detailed and offers a variety of sound theories concerning their disappearance."

"Uhhhh . . .but it's a little too thick." With his forefinger and thumb he created a gap of less than a half inch. "Do you have one about that size?"

Her face lit with an amused smile. "We do have a good children's book on the subject. It has pictures."

Wolf grinned. "To be honest with you, I don't have a lot of time. I'm on a case, and I'm trying to do a quick study on the topic."

"You're the ex-cop, aren't you?"

Wolf nodded. "I was a Dare County deputy for about five years. Now I have my own detective agency."

"Of course, I remember your face. You ran against Sheriff Walton a couple of years ago. I almost voted for you."

Wolf grimaced. "I almost thank you for your support." He held out his hand. "I'm Wes Wolf."

She shook his hand. "Jamie Hope." She swooped her arm toward the front of the store. "I manage the place."

"Nice to meet you, Jamie. What do you know about the Lost Colony?"

"I don't consider myself an authority, but I know a good bit. Give me a particular."

"Okay. Why did the English settlers come to this particular island?"

She thumbed over her shoulder toward the window. "The guy our street was named after, Sir Walter Raleigh, was commissioned by Queen Elizabeth I to establish a permanent English settlement in the New World. He didn't come in person, but he did arrange an expedition to explore this region. They arrived and discovered the surroundings here were bountiful and the natives friendly."

"So Raleigh sent over a boatload of colonists to set up camp, and then they disappeared."

"Not quite. The first colony Raleigh established was a military operation. Initially their relations with the natives were peaceful, but that didn't last. A silver cup was stolen, and the governor of the colony assumed the natives stole it. He demanded that the cup be returned. When they couldn't come up with it, he ordered that their village be burned."

"Wow. That's not a good start with your new neighbors."

"Far from it. Manteo managed to negotiate a precarious peace between the natives and the English. He suggested Roanoke Island be given to them to establish their colony."

"He's the Native American this town is named after."

She slightly closed one eye. "Right. He made a couple trips to England and became a key figure in mitigating relations between the colonists and local tribes."

"Manteo was the man to know."

She shook her head. "That's a little corny but true. The colonists heavily depended on the natives for food, but some of their leaders began to see the English as more and more of a threat. Food supplies dwindled, hostilities increased, and the colonists decided it would be best to head back to England. They made contact with Sir Francis Drake's fleet, and he offered to take them back."

Wolf chuckled. "They caught a break with Drake."

She smiled politely. "Definitely, they were lucky to escape."

"Considering the contentious relationship between the local tribes and the English, it doesn't sound like Roanoke Island was the best place to send another group of colonists."

"You're right. Sir Walter Raleigh intended to send the second group to Chesapeake Bay. One hundred and fifteen people agreed to join that colony including a pregnant young woman by the name of Eleanor Dare, her husband Ananias and father John White, who was the governor of the colony. This time the party included women and children. They weren't prepared to be thrown into an inhospitable environment like Roanoke."

"How'd they end up there?"

"Roanoke was meant to be a stop along the way to Chesapeake Bay. However, the captain of the ship, a guy by the name of Fernandes, had other plans. After dropping them off at Roanoke Island, he set sail to raid Spanish galleons along the coast. He never returned for the colonists. They were stuck at Roanoke amidst hostile tribes."

Wolf glanced out the window. The bright street had turned gray, and distant thunder rumbled. "I guess they never expected things to go so wrong so fast."

"Indeed. One of the colonists was killed by a native shortly after they arrived. Within the first month they had several skirmishes with the local tribes. Not long after that Eleanor Dare gave birth to her daughter Virginia. Eleanor's father, John White, was sent back to England on a returning ship to get help and supplies. At that time the war with Spain escalated. Travel to the New World became difficult, and White wasn't able to return to Roanoke for another three years. When he did return, the settlement had been abandoned."

Wolf rubbed his knuckles along the stubble of his jawline. "Vanished without a trace."

"Right. There are many theories explaining their disappearance, but no one knows for sure."

"What's your best guess?"

Her eyes narrowed and face muscles tensed slightly. "Well . . . I'm a realist. I believe the soundest theory is that they all perished here on Roanoke Island."

"Why do you think that?"

"They were middleclass Englanders lacking in survival skills. At the time the area was experiencing its worst drought in hundreds of years. They didn't get along with the natives but were dependent upon them for food. The natives were struggling to survive the drought themselves. Of course, there's always the threat of disease and a harsh winter. Perhaps the local tribes felt that these people from across the sea brought a curse upon the land. It's possible that fears and hostilities increased so much among the natives that they decided to wipe them out, hide their bodies and dismantle the settlement. With the evidence eliminated, the English were less likely to retaliate."

"So you believe there were no survivors."

"Correct."

"If someone came up to you and said, 'I'm a direct descendant of Eleanor Dare,' would you believe them?"

"No. To me that's an outlandish claim. If there were no survivors, then there could be no direct descendants."

"I see." Wolf glanced at the top row of books and pulled down one entitled *The Lost Colony and Their Journey to Croatoan*. "How about this book? Any good?"

The store owner took the book, turned it over and quickly read the summary on the back. "I haven't read this one, but I'm familiar with the hypothesis. Some people speculate that the colonists became desperate, headed south and somehow made it to Croatoan Island. There they intermixed with the Croatans, a friendly tribe, and assimilated into their culture."

"But you don't buy that?"

"It's a longshot possibility. When John White finally returned to the settlement, he found the word 'CROATOAN' carved into one of the posts of a palisade there. He tried to sail to the island twice, but foul weather prevented him both times."

Wolf spread his hands. "Sounds like a good possibility to me."

"My problem with the theory is there should be more archeological proof. If English settlers mixed with the Croatans, there would be loads of artifacts. However, I do know someone on the island who has written articles for the local paper about the archeological digs underway now."

"On Croatoan Island?"

"Yes, her name is Mee Mee Roberts."

"How do I get there?"

"What do you mean?"

"Do I need a boat?"

"No!" Jamie Hope laughed and clapped her hands together. "You drive over the Herbert C. Bonner Bridge. Croatoan Island is part of Dare County. It's modern day Hatteras Island."

"Oh." Wolf felt his face flush and wondered how red he looked. "See, I told you I needed professional help." He gestured toward the book she was holding. "I'll buy that one."

"Sure thing. I'll ring it up for you."

"Now *where* can I find Mee Mee Roberts?"

"She owns a bookstore in Buxton."

"That's only about forty-five minutes away. I think I'll take a quick trip down there."

She tilted her head and gave him an odd look. "It's more like an hour if you drive the speed limit."

Wolf smirked. "Who said I was going to drive the speed limit?"

Wolf decided to stop back at the office before heading down to Buxton. He trusted Angie to handle whatever complications or issues arose, but with the characters, confusion and homicides thrown into the mix of this Dare Diary case, he knew he needed to keep abreast of any new developments. Halfway across the Washington Baum Bridge the dark skies unleashed a deluge of rain, streaks of lightning and crackling thunder. By the time he turned onto Old Oregon Inlet Road, the rain had stopped, and the sun broke through the parting clouds. *August on the Outer Banks*. He parked the Cougar, snatched the new book off the seat, bounded up the steps and crossed the deck to the front door. The Wolf and Bain logo on the frosted glass caught his attention. *Wolf Detective Agency. Wolf Investigations. Wolf Detective Services.* He needed a catchy new business name. *Wolf and Stallone Detective Agency.* Hmmmm . . . Maybe.

Angie was at her computer, typing away.

"Playing Solitaire again?" Wolf asked.

She stopped and peered over her black-framed reading glasses. "No. Working on a paper — *The Basics of Crime Scene Management.*"

"If you need any professional help, let me know."

"Why? Do you know someone who could help me?"

"You're another Lucille Ball. Hey, I'm heading down to Buxton to do some research."

"Hay is for jackasses."

Wolf laughed. "I resemble that remark. Anyway, I wanted to check in with you first. Any news?"

"Your girlfriend stopped in."

"Which one?"

"Laura Bain."

"Oh no. What did you tell her?"

"I told her you went shopping for an engagement ring."

"You're on a roll today. Really, what did you tell her?"

"That you were busy with an important investigation and wouldn't be available for the next few days." She removed her reading glasses and gave Wolf a sullen stare. "She got catty with me."

"Sorry about that, Angel. She's a handful, but keep up the palisade of protection for me if at all possible."

"Palisade? Where'd you come up with that?"

"Over at Downtown Books. One of the Lost Colony members carved the word 'Croatoan' into a palisade post." He held up the book he had just purchased. "Do you know where Croatoan Island is?"

"Sure. That's where you're headed — Hatteras Island."

Wolf snickered. "Yeah. I failed that question on today's history test."

"Is that why you're going to Buxton? Learn a little history?"

"Yep. That's the plan. Anyone else stop in?

"Your two friends from the sheriff's office."

"Andy Taylor and Barney Fife?"

"Yeah. They brought a warrant with them this time."

"Well, well, well. They must have gotten the report back on the slugs they pulled out of George Bain and Frank Fregiotto."

"That would be my guess. They searched the place, but they couldn't find any guns . . . "

"I keep them well hidden."

" . . . that is except for mine."

"Did they take your Swiss and Wesson?"

"Nope." She opened the bottom drawer of her desk. "Still here."

"Guess they're not looking for a .357 Magnum."

Angie grinned like a kid who just stole the last cookie from the jar. "You're right, but I do know what calibers they are looking for."

Wolf stepped forward, his thick, rusty eyebrows hooding his eyes. "Walton told you?"

She shook her head. "Deputy Joel hung back after Walton went out the door. He asked me for a date."

"Deputy Joel, huh? First name basis. What'd you say?"

"I told him I'd let him buy me dinner if he'd tell me the caliber of the bullets they took out of the murder victims."

A smile cracked Wolf's face wide open. "You've been hanging around me too long. What were the calibers?"

Angie picked up a slip of paper from her desk. "They took a .38 out of George and a 9 mm out of Fregiotto."

Wolf snagged the scrap, took a quick glance, rolled it into a tiny ball and dropped it into the trash can next to the desk. "Angel, remind me to give you a raise as soon as I get done cashing in on this Dare Diary case."

"Forget the raise. I want a promotion."

Chapter 8

As Wolf drove to the end of East Hunter Street, he caught sight of the silver Cascada parked about forty yards up Oregon Inlet Road off to the side on the grass. Wolf turned south. *Today's the day, young Gatsby Boy. I don't know the place, but we will meet face to face.* Wolf kept glancing in his rearview mirror. The Cascada pulled out onto the highway with about two hundred yards between them. *Atta Gatsby Boy.* Old Oregon Inlet Road joined Route 12 about four miles south of Wolf's office. He turned left onto 12, and, sure enough, Gatsby Boy followed obediently.

It didn't take long from there to reach the Herbert C. Bonner Bridge, a long arch that rose up like a roller coaster across Oregon Inlet and descended to Pea Island, a narrow strip of barrier island designated as a national wildlife refuge. The view was spectacular: to the left he saw the dunes topped with seagrasses and the Atlantic Ocean, and to the right grasslands, bushes, lots of long-legged waterfowl and the Croatan Sound. The long, straight stretch of highway before him offered an excuse to ramp up the Cougar to 75 mph and see if Gatsby Boy would keep pace. He did.

Things were shaping up. Perhaps the better word would be adding up. Five thousand dollars from Virginia Dare, Two thousand seven hundred from Underdonk for setting up the meeting, and who knows what he will be able to squeeze out of Alfred Bacon. He took a quick peek in the rearview mirror. *Young Gatsby Boy will be the ticket to arranging that meeting.*

A much shorter bridge, the New Inlet Bridge, crossed the gap between Pea Island and Hatteras Island. The scenery remained pretty much the same until he passed through the town of Rodanthe, where beach houses rose up on both sides of the road. Most of them were big, six-or-seven-bedroom homes, three stories high, costing a small fortune for vacationers to rent for a week. People loved coming down here, though, and forgetting about the weary world for a while. The other small towns were similar with names like Waves, Salvo and Avon, rustic places to get away and see a different side of life on the edge of the ocean.

The village of Buxton, however, seemed more like a regular town with lots of stores, smaller homes, schools, churches, bars and cemeteries. Buxton Village Books was located about halfway through town along Route 12. Wolf pulled into the gravel parking area that lined the road to the left of the store. Two other vehicles were parked there, which left plenty of space for other customers. He exited the car and hurried to the front stoop of the shop, a quaint old one-story house painted white with black shutters. He leaned to see past a large pine tree to his right, wondering if Gatsby Boy had the cajones to pull into one of the remaining parking spaces. Nope. He turned right and drove down the road that ran along side of the store. *Very crafty. I bet he'll turn around somewhere down the road, come back this way and park out of sight. I'll catch him when I come out of the store.*

He entered the shop and took a quick look around. The owner had organized every inch of the well-stocked place. He noticed a display of local fiction directly in front of him with titles like *Murder at Hatteras*, *Murder at Whalehead*, and *Murder on the Outer Banks*. Skulls were featured on each of the covers. *Geesh. Dead bodies must be as common as seashells around here.*

"Can I interest you in a local murder mystery?" a woman's voice asked. "These are some of our bestsellers." She was a slim gal in her late fifties or early sixties. Her sandy hair was gathered into a ponytail, and her brown-framed glasses matched her summer casual midi-dress. She smiled warmly and offered her hand. "I'm Mee Mee Roberts."

"Just the lady I wanted to meet." Wolf shook her hand.

She raised her eyebrows. "Oh, really?"

"Yes. My name's Wes Wolf. I'm a private investigator with an office up in Nags Head."

She nodded slowly. "I read about a private eye that just got killed on the beach there."

"That was my partner, George Bain." He motioned at the display of murder books. "I'm not into fiction. The bullets that cut George down were very real."

The cheerful beam of her smile faded like sunshine when a thick cloud suddenly passes over. "Sorry to hear about your friend."

Wolf gave her a courteous nod. "Thanks. We weren't close friends, but we did work together for five years."

"What brings you to my shop? Is it something to do with his murder?"

"I guess in a circuitous way it does. I'm doing some research on the Lost Colony."

"Okay. Now I'm curious." She furrowed her brow. "How does a four-hundred-year-old mystery have anything to do with a recent murder?"

"You'd be surprised. I can't say more than that."

Her smile returned. "Would you like to check out our books about the Lost Colony?"

"I was hoping you could fill me in. Jamie Hope from Downtown Books told me you had a connection to the archeological digs going on down here."

"Yessiree. I've interviewed the researchers several times for articles I've written for the *Island Free Press*. You'd be amazed at some of the artifacts they've uncovered."

"That's fascinating. Jamie seems to think that the colonists all died on Roanoke Island from either being slaughtered by the local natives or starvation."

"That's the prevalent theory, but the Croatoan argument has gained more traction recently."

"She mentioned that as a possible longshot and told me about the word carved on the post—Croatoan. What do you think? Could 115 people have survived the fifty-mile trip from Roanoke to here, knowing the dangers that awaited along the way?"

Mee Mee adjusted her glasses. "The odds were against them. Many of them probably didn't survive. The relations with the local tribes were bellicose to say the least. Then they had to make two crossings from island to island over treacherous water. However, the proof is in the archeological finds."

"Why are those artifacts so important?"

Her lips tightened, and she lightly touched her hands together at the fingertips just below her chin. "If enough English artifacts are found on this island dating back to the late 1500s when the colonists would have made their journey, then there's no other explanation as to how those artifacts got here. It's the only reasonable conclusion."

"Have they found anything from that time period?"

She nodded excitedly. "A British ten-carat gold signet ring engraved with a lion and dated to the late 1500s was recently discovered near Cape Creek, which was the site of a Croatoan village. They also found a small slate used for writing and the hilt of an iron rapier that dated to that time period. The slate had the letter "M" written on one corner, and a lead pencil was found along side of it."

Wolf straightened. "That's impressive. So you think it's possible that they survived the journey and intermingled with the Croatan people?"

Mee Mee took a deep breath and let it out slowly. "I'm convinced that some of them endured the journey and joined the Croatans. The archeologists also found English pottery shards at the dig."

"But I'm guessing that Jamie would argue those items could have been traded between the natives and the English who established the first colony at Roanoke."

"That's possible, but would you trade a gold ring for a few bushels of corn?"

"If I'm hungry enough."

Mee Mee rubbed her chin. "I don't think so. But there's something else to consider. Have you ever heard of the Dare Stone?"

"No." Wolf almost said that he had heard of the Dare Diary but caught himself. *Better not let that information become public.*

"Experts can't agree on its authenticity, but it was found near Edenton, North Carolina along the Chowan River back in 1937 by a fellow named Hammond. That location was about fifty miles inland from Roanoke Island. Later a map was discovered that had been drawn by Eleanor Dare's father, John White. On the map near where the first Dare Stone was found was a symbol representing a fort. Many historians believe that White had instructed the colonists to move inland if they continued to encounter problems with the natives."

"What was on the stone?"

"Words were carved on the front and back. On the front it said, 'Ananias Dare and Virginia went to heaven— 1591.'"

"That was Eleanor's husband and daughter, correct?"

"That's right. Many experts believe that Eleanor Dare carved the stone herself. Then it said, 'Any Englishman show this rock to John White.'"

"So what do you think happened?"

"It appears that some of the colonists left Croatoan Island and traveled to the place where John White wanted to build a fort. They hoped he would come there looking for them. Archaeologists are also exploring that area for clues."

"Wow." Wolf rubbed his chin. "What did the stone say on the back?"

"It talked about sickness, suffering and war with the so called 'savages.' The natives believed that the spirits were angry. It stated that they killed all but seven of the colonists."

"You don't happen to know the names of those seven survivors, do you?"

Mee Mee tilted her head and raised a finger. "I think I have a book with their names listed." She turned a corner and disappeared down an aisle. A minute later she returned holding up a book entitled *The Unsolved Mystery of the Dare Stones*. She flipped through the pages toward the middle, displaying photographs of the stones. "As time passed, more stones were found in South Carolina. Here's the page I wanted to show you." She placed the book on the counter next to a cash register and spread the page flat. Then she ran her finger along the image of the carving. "The seven survivors are listed on this stone: William Withers, Thomas Ellis, Robert Ellis, Henry Berry, James Lacey, Eleanor Dare and the seventh name is indecipherable."

"Did you say, 'Thomas Ellis?'"

"Yes. And I believe Robert Ellis was his young son."

Wolf racked his brain. *Thomas Ellis was the name of Virginia's father. Didn't she tell me her DNA was traced through the paternal strands of the Ellis family?* "If these stones are authentic, then it's possible that Eleanor Dare survived and married one of these other men, for example Thomas Ellis?"

Mee Mee's eyes narrowed. "I would say not only possible but probable. She was young. There were no other women listed, so they must have perished. In all likelihood, she did marry one of these men and probably had children."

"Let me ask you a question. If someone came up to you and claimed to be a direct descendant of Eleanor Dare, would you believe her?"

"I'd have to see proof."

"Like a DNA analysis?"

"Right. I believe Eleanor Dare escaped Roanoke Island and lived out her life either here on Hatteras Island or somewhere in the Carolinas. If that person's DNA was traced back to Eleanor Dare or her mate, I'd certainly believe the science."

"That's fascinating. You've answered most of my questions." Wolf held out his hand. "Thanks for your time."

Mee Mee shook his hand and smiled. "Are you sure I can't interest you in a local murder mystery? The books are signed by the author."

"No, but I'll tell you what. If I solve this case, I'll write my own mystery novel."

Mee Mee gave a quick nod. "You write it, and I'll sell it."

After stepping onto the small porch that led into the bookstore, Wolf glanced to his left beyond the pine tree. He glimpsed the corner of a silver fender. He lifted his Polo shirt and unsnapped his shoulder holster. Descending the stoop, he slid his Sig Sauer out of the holster and held it against the side of his leg. He edged around the pine tree. Yep. *There he is.* The Cascada was parked along the side of the road just below the bookstore. The car wasn't idling. Wolf sidestepped onto the road and aimed his pistol at the windshield. He couldn't believe it. All he could see was the top of Gatsby Boy's Gatsby cap. Wolf approached slowly. The driver's side window was down, and the kid had nodded off. He had severe acne scars and a poor excuse for a mustache.

Wolf stuck the barrel of his handgun against his pocked cheek. He jerked awake, eyes wide and glaring at Wolf. He fumbled with his jacket pocket.

"Easy," Wolf growled. "You go for that gun, and I'll splatter your brains all over the back seat of this nice car."

Gatsby Boy froze.

"Now ease that gun out of your pocket slow as a cold snake."

He slipped his fingers into the pocket of a dark gray nylon jacket and withdrew a black handgun.

"Lay it in your lap," Wolf commanded.

The kid dropped it between his legs on the seat.

"No sudden moves." Wolf held the barrel of the Sig Sauer an inch from the thug's left eye as he retrieved the firearm. Wolf stepped back and examined the gun—a 9mm Browning Luger.

"Nice piece," Wolf said.

"I'd like to have it back," the kid growled.

"Don't get your hopes up." Wolf slid the gun into the front pocket of his black Gaberdine pants.

"You're making a big mistake, Ass-wipe."

Wolf chuckled. "I'd say that you made the big mistake by falling asleep on the job. Boss Hog Bacon won't be happy to hear about this."

The color drained from Gatsby Boy's face. "You wait," he mumbled. "Sooner or later they're gonna be picking my bullets out of your innards."

Wolf raised his rusty eyebrows. "Now that's not nice. You need to wipe your mouth after spewing that kind of crap."

The kid's whole body tensed.

"Relax. I've got a message for your boss. If he wants in on the Dare Diary, he has to go through me. Virginia Dare put me in charge. Tell him to call my office, and we'll set up a meeting real soon."

Gatsby Boy glowered at him. "What about my gun?"

"I think I'll hold on to it for a while." He thumbed over his shoulder. "Now get the hell out of here."

Gatsby Boy started the Cascada, shifted into drive and peeled out, throwing gravel at Wolf's feet.

Chapter 9

Wolf sat in his office finishing up the third chapter of *The Lost Colony and Their Journey to Croatoan*. The author made a lot of sense, adding more details to what Wolf had already discovered about the possibility of their survival. With every revelation, Virginia's claim to be a direct descendant of Eleanor Dare seemed credible. He wanted to believe her, but all her lying added a healthy portion of doubt to the plate she had handed him. He remembered their kiss at her hotel room. Despite all her flaws, he wanted her. Did he love her? She definitely knew how to raise his temperature a few degrees.

The office door opened, and Angie peeked in. "Miss Virginia Dare is here to see you."

Wolf closed the book. "I was just thinking about her. Send her in."

Virginia entered the office wearing a dark gray swing dress that flowed loosely over her lean body, swishing just above her knees. Her dark eyes were rimmed with red, and she appeared to be on the verge of crying.

"Are you all right?" Wolf asked.

She shook her head no.

He stood, and they walked toward each other, meeting in the middle of the office and clasping hands.

"What happened?"

She pulled one hand away, used her fingers to wipe the moisture from under her eyes and took a deep breath. "Someone broke into my hotel room this morning." Her voice was shaky.

"What time?"

"It must have been around ten. I went down to do a workout and take a dip in the pool. I returned about 11:30. The place was in shambles, clothes, pillows and blankets strewn all over. It looked like a whirlwind had descended. The bastard even slid the mattress off the bed."

"Looking for the diary, no doubt."

She nodded. "I don't know what I'm going to do."

"The question is: What are they willing to do?"

"Exactly. They know I don't have the diary yet."

"And only you know when and where it's arriving."

"But I won't know those exact details until my father calls me." She took in a labored breath. "Do you think they would kidnap me and torture me to get that information?"

"It's possible."

She began to sob, and Wolf wrapped his arms around her. "Take it easy. I won't let them hurt you. That's one reason you hired me."

She gazed up at him. "Please protect me," she moaned. "I'm not strong like you. I don't think I would last long under any kind of torture."

He rubbed her back and kissed her forehead in hopes of calming her. After a few minutes she regained some control and breathed haltingly.

"It can't be Underdonk," Wolf said. "He wants to make up with you."

She shook her head. "I'm not afraid of Underdonk. It's Alfred Bacon and his creepy nephew, Willard Bacon. Willard will do anything for him."

"Even murder?"

Her eyes filled with dread. "He'd kill without hesitation."

Wolf released her and stood back. "I don't understand. Originally, you planned on selling the diary to Bacon. Why would you want to deal with a man like that?"

She looked at the ceiling and gasped a quick breath. "He lives by his own moral code and doesn't veer from it. That sounds odd, but it's true. I've dealt with him before without any problems. He quoted me a reasonable price for the diary, and my father and I agreed to it. If Frank would have kept his nose out of it and let me handle it, there wouldn't have been a problem. I would have picked up the diary, delivered it, and he would have paid me the money, no questions asked."

"How much did he offer?"

She focused on Wolf, her dark eyes cold and intent. "Five million dollars."

"Whoa. Are you serious?"

She nodded.

"How much could he get for it?"

"Who knows? Maybe twenty million or more."

"So when Freggiotto invited Underdonk to the party, he became angry."

"Livid. He believed we had a solid deal. With Underdonk in on the bidding, the price would go up. He considered that a betrayal and doesn't tolerate any kind of disrespect. Now he feels justified to take the diary from me one way or the other, and young Willard will do his bidding." She lowered her head

Wolf reached and clasped her shoulders. "Look at me."

Virginia raised her head, and their eyes met.

"I promise you that he will not harm you. Let me handle Bacon and Gatsby Boy. That's what I call young Willard. I already took his gun from him."

Her eyes widened. "You did?"

With eyes fixed on her, he raised and lowered his head. "I expect to meet with Bacon soon. When I do, I will lay down the law. If he wants to buy the diary, he'll play by my rules." Wolf rubbed his chin. "And he'll pay top market price."

"But . . . but . . ." her voice trembled, "he might try to kill you."

Wolf grinned devilishly. "Let him try. I didn't go into this business to be safe and sound. Hell no. I'm here to make a profit, and that requires risk." He raised his chin and drew his finger across his neck. "The risk factor on this case has just gone up a couple notches. I don't expose myself to these kinds of hazards at bargain-basement prices. I want a percentage of the sale."

She tightened her lips and bobbed her head slowly. "I guess that's . . . that's only fair. How much . . . how much of a percentage do you want?"

"The normal agent's cut—fifteen percent."

She exhaled audibly. "Okay. I know I won't survive without you." She reached and cupped the sides of his face in her hands. "I'm trusting you to protect me and make the sale for me. You won't betray me, will you?"

"No Ma'am. I live by my own moral code, too. If I make a promise, I will follow through on it."

"If we both agree, then let's seal this contract with a kiss." She drew his face down to her.

Wolf pressed his lips on hers. They were warm and moist and wonderful. Her hands slid behind his head, her fingers interlacing. He slid his hand down her back, cupped her behind and drew her hard against him.

The office door swung open, and a women's voice cried, "What's going on!"

They broke apart and turned toward the voice, breathing at a rapid pace.

Laura Bain stood in the doorway, visibly shaking. She wore a black maxi dress with a low V-cut neckline.

Angie's face appeared in the opening behind her. "I'm sorry, Wes, but I told her you were with a client. When she heard Miss Dare's voice, she charged right in."

"How could you do this?" Laura fumed.

Wolf took a step toward her, raised his hand and said, "Stop right there. I told you yesterday that our affair had been a mistake."

Laura's red-rimmed mouth opened like a gaping wound. "You said the night we shared was a night to remember!" Her lips trembled as she spoke. "You said you needed time!"

"You're only hearing what you want to hear, Laura," Wolf's voice remained cool and aloof. "I've had enough time to think. We had one night together and that's all it took. It's over between us. It barely began." He pointed at the door. "I want you out of here. Out of my life."

Her eyes grew wide, the whites like three-quarter moons above her irises. "You son of a bitch! You dirty son of a bitch!" Her shaking hands balled into fists. "I'll get even with you. Wait and see. I'm going to destroy you!"

Angie clasped Laura's shoulder. "Mrs. Bain, you need to leave."

She ripped herself away from Angie's grasp. "Don't touch me! Don't come near me!" She took a deep breath and glared one last time at Wolf with flaming eyes. "I'm sending you to hell." She spun away, marched passed Angie, across the outer office and out the front door.

Angie knotted her brow and patted her chest. "Don't blame this on me."

Wolf raised his hands. "It's not your fault. It's my fault."

Virginia, her face aghast, said "Who was that?"

"Laura Bain, George's wife," Wolf muttered.

Virginia's eyes narrowed. "You told me their marriage was rocky, but you never said that you were the reason."

"Don't jump to conclusions. She and George talked divorce for years. They just never got around to it."

"What do you think she's going to do?" Angie said. "If she shot George, she'd have no qualms about shooting you."

"She didn't shoot George, and she's not going to shoot me. She'll get over it. Do you think I'm her first one-night stand? No way. It won't be long, and she'll be on the prowl for another sucker."

Virginia laid her palm against her forehead. "I need to sit down."

"That's a good idea." Wolf motioned toward his swivel chair. "Take a seat. I need to have a private word with Angie."

Virginia slumped into Wolf's chair, and he ushered Angie into the outer office and closed the door.

"Listen," he said, "I need a big favor."

Angie's bright blue eyes clouded over. "What kind of favor?"

"I want you to let Virginia stay at your place for a couple days."

"Weston, you know I don't trust her." Her voice was low but harsh.

"That's a good thing. Neither do I. I don't want you to feel comfortable around her. She's in big trouble. Bad people are after her. I need you to be vigilant."

"I don't know about this."

"You said you wanted to be my partner, right?"

She took a sharp breath and let it out. "Yeah."

"Well . . . I want a partner who can roll with the punches."

She gave Wolf a withering stare. "Okay. I'll do it, but I'm not looking forward to it."

"That's my girl."

She grabbed Wolf by collar with both hands. "I'm not your girl. I'm your next partner."

Wolf slowly pried her hands away. "We'll see how this goes. There's something else."

"What!"

"I don't want Virginia driving around in that Mercedes. I'm going to hide it out back. Can you borrow your mother's car and let her drive yours?"

"I guess so."

"Good. I'm going to send her over there with you now." He thumbed over his shoulder. "Go get her. I need to step outside and make sure Gatsby Boy isn't lurking on the corner."

Angie headed back into Wolf's office, and he walked out onto the front deck. He scanned the area but didn't see the silver Cascada or anyone who appeared suspicious. When Virginia came through the door and stood beside him, he went over his plan to move her to Angie's house. They transferred her baggage into the trunk of Angie's green Honda Civic, and Wolf moved her Mercedes to the back of the bungalow. When he returned, she and Angie stood, waiting by the driver's side door.

Wolf placed his hand on Virginia's shoulder. "I want you to listen carefully. On the way over to Angie's, lie down in the back seat so no one can see you. I don't want to take any chances. Tonight, when you come back here for the meeting with Underdonk, wear a scarf or a big hat—anything to cover most of your head. We've only got a couple days before the diary arrives. You need to be cautious and lay low." Wolf opened the car door and folded the seat over so Virginia could climb into the back. Then he turned and embraced her.

She gave him a quick peck on the lips. "Thank you for watching over me."

"You better thank Angie. This plan wouldn't work without her cooperation."

She reached and clasped Angie's hand. "Thanks, Angie. You're a lifesaver."

Angie shook off her hand and said, "Get in the car. I want to drop you off and get back here. I've got work to do."

Virginia's eyes flashed with hurt, but she obediently crawled into the back seat. Angie lowered herself into the front seat and started the car. Wolf closed the door, and Angie glared at him through the glass. Then she backed out and drove away.

Wolf rubbed his chin as he watched the Civic turn the corner onto Old Oregon Inlet Road. *Five million, dollars and it could be worth twenty or thirty. No sir, Boss Hog Bacon. Five million won't do. If you want the diary, you better be ready to reach farther into those deep pockets.*

Chapter 10

Underdonk arrived fifteen minutes early for the meeting. Wolf greeted him at the front door and ushered him into his office, leaving his office door open. Underdonk wore the same indigo-violet suit but added a black bowler hat with a yellow feather tucked into the band and a black cane to his accessories. Wolf had separated the two wooden armchairs in front of his desk so that there was plenty of space between them. Underdonk sat in the one closest to the far wall, his legs barely long enough to plant his alligator shoes flat on the floor.

"Nice hat," Wolf said.

Underdonk lifted the front by the brim an inch or so and lowered it. "Your compliment is acknowledged with gratitude." He leaned his cane against Wolf's desk.

"Would you like a glass of wine?"

"That would be most helpful."

An oversized bottle of Cabernet Sauvignon sat next to three long-stemmed glasses on Wolf's desk. He turned over two of the glasses and filled them a little over halfway with the red wine. He handed one to Underdonk and took a long drink from the other.

Underdonk lifted the glass. "Wine, the duct tape of the soul." He took a sip.

"Any problems with Mr. Bacon and his nephew Willard lately?"

"I haven't seen either one," Underdonk wheezed. He sipped the wine again as he rested his free hand on his paunch. "I don't think Bacon is out to get me."

"You may be right. You didn't break the agreement he had made with Miss Dare."

"That's true. I just accepted an invitation."

"I'm guessing that's why Frank Fregiotto is no longer with us—a broken contract."

"Poor Frank. He was seduced by the root of all evil."

"From what Miss Dare tells me, there is a lot of money to be made for the one who is willing to dig deep for that root."

"That depends on the costs of doing business."

"Are you willing to take a chance?"

He tapped the top of the bowler. "If the diary is authentic, I will throw my hat into the ring."

"Certainly, you've seen pictures and other proofs of its authenticity, or you wouldn't be here."

"I've seen the diary in person and the certified analysis reports provided by Miss Dare's father, Mr. Ellis. The diary is authentic, but before I bid, I want to make sure the one that's delivered is the one I saw."

"I don't blame you. If it is the real McCoy, some experts would say that it's priceless."

He smiled oddly, his thin mustache forming a batlike shape. "Don't believe the experts. Everything can be bought for a price."

"Let's hope Miss Dare graciously extends you that opportunity."

The glimmer of confidence faded from his face, his eyes lowering and smile sagging into a frown. "Yes, let's hope."

"Why does she hate you so much?"

He raised his head and met Wolf's gaze. "She believes I killed her brother."

Wolf stiffened, feeling a chill at the back of his neck. "I wasn't expecting that answer."

Underdonk shrugged. "It is what it is."

The outer office door opened, and Virginia Dare entered wearing a flower-print wrap scarf over her hair and tied beneath her chin. She had on jeans and a crimson tunic top. She closed the door behind her.

Wolf hurried through his office and into the outer room to greet her. "How are things going at Angie's place?"

"Chilly," she said, "but safe."

"That's the operative word—safe. Chilly but safe is better than warm but dangerous."

"I won't argue with you on that point."

Wolf led her into his office, closed the door and motioned toward the empty chair. "Have a seat." She lowered herself onto the armchair. He turned over the other glass, filled it half full with wine and handed it to her. "Drink up. It will help you relax." She sipped the wine as Wolf eased onto his swivel chair and scooted behind the scarred wooden desk.

Underdonk bowed his head. "Miss Dare, thank you for graciously agreeing to meet with me."

She gave him a cold stare. "If it were up to me, we would not be meeting."

"I insisted on the meeting," Wolf said. "Virginia agreed only at my behest."

"Yes," Underdonk said, "You do have extraordinary persuasive skills."

Wolf smiled cordially. "I guaranteed you a meeting with Miss Dare, and here we are. You got what you paid for. Now it's up to you to convince her to invite you to the sale."

Underdonk shifted his focus in her direction. "Well, Miss Dare, my argument is fairly simple. I'm willing to double Bacon's first offer. If money talks, you'll invite me to the auction. If not, I'll be on my way."

Virginia's hard-lined face softened. "You're willing to double the offer? Do you even know how much he offered me?"

"Knowing Bacon, I could make an educated guess—four or five million."

She raised her eyebrows. "Good guess. He offered five million. Is ten million your limit?"

"I doubt if he'll bid more than that."

The iciness returned to her features. "You understand, Mr. Underdonk, that if you are invited, then we will entertain offers from both of you. The bidding may go way beyond ten million."

Underdonk rubbed the jade stone on his ring. "I'm prepared to go higher if need be."

"Hmmmm." She nodded slowly, thoughtfully. "There's just one more thing you must do before I invite you to the sale."

"And that is . . . ?"

"You must apologize to me for killing my brother."

Underdonk's mouth dropped open, and his eyes bulged. "But I . . . I . . ."

A hard rapping erupted from the front office door, and all three of them flinched and turned in the direction of the clamor.

Wolf shot to his feet and extended his hands in front of him. "Stay put. Keep quiet. I'll see who it is and send them on their way."

He stepped out of his office, closed the door and strode across the room to the frosted entryway. Two blurry figures stood on the other side of the glass. He opened the door a few inches to see Deputy Joel Thomas and Sheriff Dugan Walton. "To what do I owe this unexpected visit from Dare County's finest?"

"Hi, Wes," Deputy Thomas said. "Can we step in and talk to you."

"Sorry, Joel, but I'm very busy tonight."

"This won't take long," Sheriff Walton snarled.

"You'll have to come back tomorrow." Wolf began to close the door, but Walton stuck his foot in the gap.

"We'd tried to be nice," Walton said, "but, as usual, you don't give a rat's ass. Either let us in and answer some questions, or we'll read you your rights and haul you over to the station in Manteo."

Wolf opened the door a few more inches. "Are you serious?"

"More serious than a tight-rope walker on a windy day."

Wolf swung the door open, and the two lawmen entered. Then he slammed the door with a loud clap. "What's this all about?"

Walton smiled smugly. "About an hour and a half ago your departed partner's poor widow stopped by my office."

Wolf closed his eyes. *Oh no. This can't be good.* "What did she say about me?"

"She claimed that you and she have been dancing in the sheets for some time behind her husband's back. Is that true?"

"No."

Walton's eyes appeared to glow with devilment. "She said it's true. She said she tried to end it, but you had fallen too hard for her."

Wolf laughed. "She's lying, and you know it."

"I don't know it. She said that you were so obsessed with her that you killed her husband so that you could marry her."

Wolf took a step back and grinned. "Make up your mind. Did I kill Fregiotto to revenge my partner's death, or did I kill my partner so that I could live my life in misery married to a sausage jockey?"

Walton shook his head. "That's not a nice thing to say. Deputy Thomas, read him his rights."

Thomas stepped forward, withdrew a white card from his pants pocket and began to read: "You have the right . . . "

Wolf held up one hand like a traffic cop. "Wait a minute now. You boys know Laura Bain's reputation. It's her word against mine. This kind of evidence is more flimsy than a kindergarten paper chain. What do you really want?"

Walton held up two fingers. "Two things. And I promise we will put your ass behind bars tonight and keep you there unless you give them to us."

"I'm listening."

"First . . .," Walton poked Wolf's side where the Sig Sauer was strapped. ". . . we'll take that heater you've got hidden under your blouse."

Wolf unbuttoned his denim shirt and exposed the gun. "Take it. I didn't shoot anybody."

"Sorry about this, Wes." Deputy Thomas slipped the card back into his pocket, unhitched the holster and withdrew the gun.

"What else?" Wolf snapped.

"Second . . .," Walton raised two fingers again. ". . . we want the name of the client who hired you to trail Fregiotto."

"I can't give that to you."

"Fine. Deputy Thomas, read him his rights."

Thomas gave Walton a sideways glance and fished into his pocket again for the card. "You have the right to remain . . ."

A loud scream pierced the air, and a man's voice shouted, "Stop it! Stop it! You're hurting me!"

Walton riveted his eyes on Wolf's office door. "What's going on in there?"

Wolf sprung toward his office, slung open the door and snagged the cane in midair. Virginia's momentum jolted to a stop. She turned and tried to yank it from his hands.

Underdonk cried, "Don't let her hit me again!"

"Whoa! Whoa!" Walton shouted. "Enough of this!"

She let go of the cane. "He . . . he . . . he . . ." Virginia's face had turned crimson, matching her top. She blinked several times, shifting her eyes from Wolf to Walton to Thomas.

"He what!" Sheriff Walton demanded

"He is a bastard." She took a deep breath, and the blood drained from her face.

Underdonk sat up and straightened his suit jacket.

Walton pivoted and faced Wolf. "What's going on here?"

Wolf grinned. "I can explain everything . . ."

Walton crossed his arms. "I'm waiting."

Wolf spread his arms. "I invited two of my friends over for some drinks and a game of . . . uh . . . charades. You know how heated a game of charades can get."

"That's r-r-right," Virginia sputtered. "I've had too much to d-d-drink and lost my temper over a silly game."

Walton lowered his thick reddish eyebrows. "Charades! I know a charade when I see one. Who are these people?"

Wolf slipped his arm around Virginia's waist. "This is my girlfriend, Emma Ritz." He waved the cane toward Underdonk. "And this is one of my clien . . . I mean associates, Hugh Underdonk."

Walton's snarl turned into a sly smile. "One your associates, huh?" He glanced at Deputy Thomas and then back at Wolf.

"That's right."

Walton faced the diminutive man. "Mr. Underdonk, did you know a guy by the name of Frank Fregiotto?"

Underdonk searched the floor as if he were looking for lost a cufflink. "Why . . . yes. I did know Frank. He was a . . . an acquaintance of mine."

"We're investigating his murder," Walton said. "We'd like you to come over to the office in Manteo and answer a few questions."

Underdonk peered up at the sheriff. His eyes widened, eyelids tensing. "I . . . I don't know anything about his murder."

"Nevertheless, we still want you to come with us and answer some questions."

Underdonk swiveled his head. "No. I don't want to go."

"If you refuse," Walton said, "then you will become a prime suspect in the murder case."

Underdonk's eyes watered. He heaved a few breaths. "Okay. I'll go with you, but I'm telling you the truth. I don't know anything about his murder."

Wolf extended the hook end of the cane to Underdonk and helped pull him up and out of the chair. As he passed, Wolf handed him his cane, bent over and whispered, "Keep your mouth shut."

Underdonk gave him a hangdog look and nodded.

"What did you say to him?" Walton asked.

Wolf straightened. "I apologized for your rude intrusion on this man's privacy."

Walton clamped his hand on Underdonk's shoulder. "No apology needed. We're just doing our job." He directed the penguin-like fellow toward the door. As they passed into the outer office Walton piped, "Thanks, Wolf. We got what we came for."

Deputy Thomas followed them but stopped and turned at the doorway. "Sorry about all of this, Wes."

"It's not your fault, Joel."

"Could you do me a favor?"

"Sure thing."

"Tell Angie I said hi, and I'm looking forward to our date on Saturday afternoon."

"Will do. Just make sure you treat her like a lady."

Deputy Thomas smiled. "Oh, I will. You can count on that." He hustled through the front office and out the door to catch up with the sheriff and Underdonk.

Wolf turned and faced Virginia. "I want to know what happened to your brother. And don't lie to me."

Chapter 11

Virginia untied the knot under her chin and removed the flowered scarf. She let it fall onto Wolf's desk, and it sat there like a deflated colorful pyramid. She lifted the half-full wine glass and emptied it with several gulps. Glancing around the room, she appeared to be lost or trapped and looking for a way to escape. "Let's get out of this office," she murmured.

Wolf snagged the wine bottle with one hand and their two empty glasses with the other. "Follow me." He led her out of the office and down the hallway to his bedroom. He set the glasses on the bedside table and turned on the lamp. "Have a seat." He motioned to a well-worn wingback armchair in the corner.

She settled onto the chair. "Figures you'd lead me to your bedroom."

Filling the wine glasses, he said, "This cottage has five rooms—two offices, a kitchen, a bathroom and a bedroom. Maybe one day, if I get lucky, I'll upgrade, but for now, this is it."

"This will do." She glanced out the window as the curtains fluttered from the breeze off the ocean. "Nice view, anyway."

Wolf handed her the glass of wine. "I like it. The sea doesn't give a damn. It's brutal. I like the sound of it, the smell of it. It reminds me we're here for a moment, and then we're gone."

She sighed. "Like my brother Robert."

"Tell me what happened."

The lamplight created a clash of light and shadow on her pale face. "It's a long and painful story."

He sat down on the bed. "I've got all night."

She took a sip of wine. "We were twins. When we were eight years old, our mother died of pancreatic cancer. It was a horrible period of my life, those six months watching her suffer. Father did his best, but he was an obsessive man."

"Obsessed with what?"

"Junk. He was what is known as a picker. He traveled around the southeast looking for antiques and oddities. We had a store in downtown Charlotte. Barely paid our bills month by month. Every once in a while, he'd strike gold and find a rare object. That's how we met Bacon and Underdonk. They dealt in antiquities and competed for our best items. The payoff was good. We'd live like kings for a few weeks, but then it was back to the grind. As we grew older, he'd take Robert with him, and I'd mind the store. I knew Robert was his favorite. He was my favorite, too. Sometimes it felt like we competed for Robert's attention."

"Sounds like you spent a lot of time by yourself."

"I did. At times it was lonely but at other times glorious. Lonesome people make choices: either you curl up into a ball and feel sorry for yourself or stand up and confront the rotten world. I decided to battle the world, most of the time anyway."

"I noticed you do have a hard edge. I saw it in the manner you were thumping Underdonk with that cane."

She laughed. "He deserved it. He apologized to me, but I could tell he wasn't sincere. He said that Robert's death was partially his fault but mostly Robert's. That's when I picked up the cane and started pounding him."

"I'm sure you left your mark on him."

"Several."

"So is he in or out?"

"I don't know." She studied the ceiling. "He's wealthier than Alfred Bacon. Ten million is nothing to blow your nose at. During my younger years, I'd pick pennies off the sidewalk to get enough money to buy a candy bar. I just hope Bacon doesn't freak out if Underdonk shows up at the table."

"Bacon took out Fregiotto. Maybe that satisfied his sense of moral injustice."

"To some degree. However, Frank's murder may have been Bacon's warning to Underdonk to get out of town."

"I'm not afraid of going head to head with Bacon. He's got a triggerman with a high handicap. If I were you, I'd bet on me. Underdonk doesn't even seem too worried about him."

Concern etched slight lines at the corners of her mouth and eyes. "I hope you're right. His nephew's incompetency doesn't diminish his mean streak. Underdonk would be a fool to let his guard down. Anyway, thanks for deflecting attention away from me and on to Underdonk."

Wolf grinned, remembering Walton taking the bait. "I didn't even have to lie to pull that one off. Underdonk really is my client." Wolf took a big swig of wine and wiped his mouth with his other hand. "However, you do need to make a decision. I plan on stopping by Underdonk's hotel tomorrow to let him know one way or the other."

Virginia twirled her finger. "What the hell. Let him in."

"I think that's a good decision." Wolf set his wine glass on the nightstand. *A perfect decision. I can hear the cash register bells ringing already.* "Okay, that's that. Let's get back to your story."

She inhaled slowly and let the breath out even more slowly. "If you insist."

"I do."

"My father had another obsession: ancestry. I remember his conversations with my mother about his unwavering conviction that we were descendants of the Lost

Colony. His name, Thomas Ellis, matched one of the names of the colonists. He named Robert after that colonist's son and me after Virginia Dare. When the genealogy companies became popular, he signed up immediately. He spent hours and hours on the ancestry websites. He read all the history books on the subject. He even went to Brenau University in Georgia to see the Dare Stones in person."

Wolf straightened and leaned forward on the bed. "I've read about the Dare Stones. One of them listed seven survivors including Thomas Ellis, his son Robert and Eleanor Dare."

She tilted her head. "I'm impressed. You've done your homework. I'm sure that's where Father got the idea to name us. He assumed Eleanor married Thomas Ellis and continued the family line through their offspring. According to the first Dare Stone, Eleanor's daughter Virginia died young at the hands of the natives." Her focus drifted from Wolf to a dark corner of the room. "Being her namesake, I've often wondered if I'll die young."

"That's silly," Wolf said. "I don't believe in omens, superstitions, karma or prophecies. Life just happens."

She met his gaze again. "And so does death."

"Right, but death doesn't count on a black cat crossing your path or seeing the image of the Grim Reaper in a pancake you just turned over. Death comes indifferently."

"Like a bullet to the heart?"

Wolf nodded. "That's one way. Is that how Robert died?"

"No. He died with a noose around his neck."

"Suicide?"

She stared at him, as if she could see into the dark recesses of his soul where he kept his secrets hidden. "Robert was twenty years old when he came out. Of course, I knew all along that he was gay. Father pretended to be supportive, but I could tell it bothered him. They spent less time together traveling the backroads looking for rusty gold. Things flipflopped. Robert spent more time at the store, and I went picking with Father. I must admit that I was pretty good at it. I struck some major finds, and Robert was gifted at dealing with customers. The business grew, and Father hired Frank as a utility man. He was a decent picker and could run the store when Robert went out of town. Our income almost doubled, and we lived comfortably for the first time in our lives.

"Underdonk was twenty years older than my brother, but Robert was impressed by his wealth and extravagant lifestyle. He made several major sales to Underdonk, and they started seeing each other regularly. Underdonk kept an apartment in Charlotte, and Robert would stay there with him often. I could tell their relationship had a detrimental impact on Robert, but he wouldn't listen to reason. Despite the increased profits, life wasn't the same for Father and me. Work was the only bright spot in our lives. Things came crashing down when Robert died, . . . but then I remembered finding the diary."

"You found the diary?"

She nodded. "I didn't know it at the time. I was only ten years old."

"Where did you find it?"

"A couple years after my mother died, my father rented an old, run down Colonial house in the historic district of Charlotte. It was a creepy old place, drafty and full of cobwebs. It had six bedrooms, a big attic and a dungeon of a basement. In the evenings Father spent time going from room to room, cleaning and straightening. At least that's what I thought he was doing. It was the perfect place to play hide and seek. Sometimes it took me thirty minutes to find Robert. He would hide under a bed or in a closet of one of the upstairs bedrooms. Whenever I would hide, Robert seemed to find me within ten minutes."

Wolf chuckled. "And you didn't like your brother one-upping you."

She smiled and took a sip of wine. "That's right. You're getting to know me. One day I decided to hide in the attic. Father forbid us to go up there because of the bats. To me it was worth the chance to get an edge on Robert. The attic was on the third floor. I crept up the stairs and creaked open the door. It was a large, musty room. Dust motes floated through the light rays filtering through the two sullied windows. A few coat racks stood against the walls with old shirts and dresses on wire hangers. Some boxes were strewn here and there on the floor and stacked against the wall. Other than that, there wasn't much up there. But then I noticed a door off to the side. I opened it to find a good-sized closet — the perfect hiding place. I left the door slightly ajar to provide some light. Then I sat against the back wall, waiting and waiting and waiting. Finally, after about forty-five minutes, I heard footsteps and saw the beam of a flashlight. Robert opened the door and shined the light directly into my face. 'Found you,' he said. I told him, 'But I win.' I started to get up, and he said, 'You cheated. We're not allowed up here.' Then he pushed me back down. My back hit the wall and something broke loose. I tumbled backward into darkness."

Wolf leaned forward, elbows on his knees. "You fell through the wall?"

She nodded. "A panel had broken loose, and I landed in between the timbers of the roof gables. I managed to catch the back of my arms on the joists. The only thing holding me besides the joists was the plaster lathe of the ceiling below me. Looking up into the darkness, I could make out the rafters. Robert grabbed my arms and pulled me back through the rectangular hole into the closet. I snatched his flashlight, spun around and directed the beam into the cavern. We saw the underside of the roof slanting down to a large brick chimney.

A wooden box was propped against the chimney, its base sitting on one of the timbers."

"Whoa!" Wolf held up his hands as if a preoccupied person was about to run into him. "So this was a secret panel?"

"Yes. Someone had purposely sealed it so you could not tell it could be used to access the space. I wanted to see what was in that box. I gave Robert the flashlight and he kept the beam fixed on it. I crawled to it, keeping my feet and hands on the two joists. When I got to the chimney, I heard rustling. I glanced around the drafty space but couldn't see anything with the limited light. I managed to slide the top off the box off. Inside was a leatherbound book with a strap around it. I could tell it was ancient."

"The Dare Diary?"

"Yes."

"Why did somebody hide it there?"

"I didn't find that out for years to come."

"Did you take it with you?"

"No. I managed to put the lid back on and prop it against the chimney. Then I heard the rustling noise again. Bats! They started flying all around me. I kept batting them away. One got stuck in my hair, and I struggled to untangle it. Somehow, inch by inch, I managed to back my way out. Robert slid the panel out through the opening and pressed it against the hole. We'd broken the seal, but we knew we had to secure it to the wall to keep the bats from entering the attic. I remembered the boxes. I rushed into the outer room and dragged several boxes into the closet. They were filled with old clothes and knickknacks. We stacked them on top of each other in front of the panel."

"Did you tell your father about the book?"

"Not then. We didn't want to get in trouble. Not long after that we moved back to the old neighborhood. I did tell him fifteen years later."

"Geesh." Wolf ran his hands over his unruly hair, somewhat flattening the curls behind his ears. "You kept that to yourself for fifteen years?"

"Remember, I had no idea it was the Dare Diary. For all I knew, it was just an old book." She held up her wine glass. "I need a refill."

Wolf gripped the neck of the bottle, stood, leaned in her direction and filled the glass in her outreached hand. "That's your third one. Remember, you've got to drive back to Angie's tonight."

She waved her hand carelessly. "I'm as sober as a Southern Baptist."

"So when did you tell your father about the diary?"

"The day after Robert died, almost one year ago. The police were obtuse about the whole investigation. They found him hanging in Underdonk's apartment. All they would commit to was a possible suicide. Robert was a very sensitive man, and Underdonk a very selfish man. Something happened between them that pushed Robert off the edge."

"Did he leave a suicide note?"

"No. I found that very suspicious. The police wouldn't give me many details, and my father didn't want to talk about it. Underdonk said it was an accident. How could hanging yourself be an accident? Throughout our lives, we kept each other sane. Underdonk led him astray. Robert followed him along the jagged edge of indulgence and instability. He did something to cause Robert to fall off that edge." She swallowed and gritted her teeth. "I wanted to bash his head in with that cane tonight."

Wolf noticed her rigid jaw and a blue vein rising on her forehead. *Whew, she has a temper. All that wine should have kicked in by now.* He said, "Sometimes you just have to let things go."

She closed her eyes, and the vein faded into her pale complexion. "It's hard."

"No charges were filed against Underdonk?"

She swiveled her head and frowned. "The superrich slide from judgment like an omelet from a Teflon pan." She blinked her watery eyes several times and glanced around the room. A tear traced a wet line down her cheek. "The next day Father and I sat in the kitchen, eating potato salad that a neighbor had sent over. We began to reminisce about the good old days with Robert. That's when I told him about finding the leatherbound book in the rafters of that old colonial house."

"What did he do?"

"He almost fell off the stool."

"He knew that you had found the diary?"

She nodded. "Back then I thought he was cleaning and straightening up the rooms to make the place livable for us. He was actually searching for the diary. He knew it was in that house."

"How did he know?"

"Through his investigation into our ancestry he discovered a great uncle named Raymond Ellis. The old fart was one hundred and two years old with a mind as sharp as a barber's razor. He was living in a nursing home in Raleigh, and Father made several trips to visit him. Uncle Raymond told him that his great grandfather, Charles Ellis, hid the diary in that house in the mid-1800s. The diary had been stored in a wooden box and placed in the bottom of a trunk. The trunk had been passed down through the generations without much thought of what it contained. When his great grandfather discovered the book, he wasn't exactly sure what he had found. Of course, Eleanor Dare penned the words using the language of her time, Elizabethan English. Those words were hard to read and understand. Doing research in those days took time and great effort. There was no internet or History Channel. Libraries weren't that common. He took the diary to a local historian, and he shed some light on its origin."

Wolf poured himself another glass of wine and took a slow sip. "I would think that even back then there would be great interest in a find of this magnitude."

"There was." She shifted in the chair, placing both elbows on the armrests and templing her hands. "Word spread. Charles began to receive requests from interested parties to see the diary. He was a naturally suspicious man, but his suspicion turned into paranoia. He wouldn't show it to anyone and worried that he may be pressured to hand it over to the government. He realized it was a fundamental record of the founding of America. He feared people in power may use questionable legal means to get their hands on it. After someone tried to break into the house, he decided to hide it in the rafters of the attic. The rumors of the diary slowly faded into legend. By the time he told his great grandson about it, he was in the throes of dementia. He knew he had hidden it somewhere in the house but couldn't remember where."

Wolf set the glass on the nightstand and planted his hands on his knees. "And there it sat against the chimney for one hundred and fifty years until you found it. That's an incredible story."

"You don't believe in fate, do you?"

"No, but I do believe in coincidence."

She pointed to her chest. "I'm Virginia Dare Ellis. I'm a direct descendant of Eleanor Dare Ellis. I was meant to find that diary by the gods of history."

Wolf eyed her, thinking she was the strangest but most beautiful woman he had ever known. "I'm Weston Wolf," he said. "I'm nobody special, but for some reason I'm here. Did we meet by coincidence or fate? Take your pick."

"Fate. And you have been appointed by the gods to help me pull this off."

Wolf laughed with a roaring laughter that shook the bed and nightstand, making the wineglass rattle.

Virginia joined him, seemingly swept up in his exhilaration. "Don't you believe me?" she said between fits of laughter.

He settled himself and met her gaze. "I don't have to believe you. You hired me to do a job, and I'll do it. Now I know why this sale is so secretive."

Her lips tightened and eyes narrowed. "Obviously, if we wanted the diary, we had to steal it."

"Who broke into the house?"

"Frank Frigiotto."

"So good old Frank did the deed."

"Yes, and the next morning the police came knocking on our door."

"Nooooo!" Wolf rubbed his knuckles along his jawline, feeling the roughness of his beard. "How'd he get caught?"

"Someone had purchased the old house and was in the process of renovating the place. We didn't know security cameras had be installed. They had video evidence of Frank leaving with the wooden box."

"Geesh! Apparently, you Houdini-ed your way out of that somehow."

"My father came up with a story. He told them we had lived in the house years ago and had stored a rare book in the attic inside of a wooden box— a pristine copy of Faulkner's *The Sound and the Fury*, the 1929 first edition. When someone came into the store and asked for a copy, he couldn't find it. Then he remembered where he'd put it. He told them he sent Frank to get it, believing he had a right to retrieve his property."

Wolf chuckled. "Did they fall for it?"

"Not at first. The owners weren't satisfied and still insisted on pressing charges."

"Sounds like a game of chess. What was his next move?"

"He offered to give them the Faulkner first edition if they dropped the charges. The novel was worth ten thousand dollars."

A smile spread across Wolf's face. "I'm impressed. Your dad is crafty as a fox." He shifted his hands back and forth in a circular motion. "The old shell game except with rare books instead of marbles. I'm guessing they dropped the charges?"

With her elbow on the arm of the chair, she unfolded her hand in his direction. "They went from seeing themselves as crime victims to seeing dollar signs."

"Ben Franklin can be quite convincing when he stares you in the face."

Virginia gave him a sly smile. "You should know."

"Ha!" He pressed his hand to his heart. "You got me. By the way, wasn't *The Sound and the Fury* about a dysfunctional southern family?"

"Yeah. The perfect book for us to trade for the Dare Diary."

"That was some trade, though: ten thousand for ten million. Of course, if you could hold a public auction, you'd probably get thirty million."

"Or more, but that's not possible. The homeowners would hear about it and become suspicious. In the eyes of the law, we stole it from them."

"Let's not let legalities spoil our plans."

"Never." She stood and wobbled slightly before catching her balance. "I guess I am a little woozy." She staggered to the bed and placed her hands on his shoulders. "Can you think of something we can do for the next hour to help sober me up?"

He clasped his hands around the small of her back and pulled her to him, using her momentum to drive them backwards onto the bed. She lay on top of him, her hands pressed flat against the mattress, one on each side of his head.

"I knew you'd think of something," she said. She lowered herself and kissed him softly twice and then more hungrily.

He wrapped his arms around her and rolled over so that he was on top. The quick turnabout caused her to let out a soft moan. "Of course, I would come up with something," he said. "Friends don't let friends drive drunk."

Chapter 12

Wolf awakened alone at nine 'o clock on Friday morning. He lay on his back, remembering the passionate moments of caressing, kissing, searching, exploring, yielding, moaning, dominating, peaking and descending. Playing the scene over on the screen of his mind, he reached and placed his hand flat on the other side of the bed where she had lain next to him. But the sheet was cold, and he felt abandoned. He didn't like this feeling that had come over him. With all the other women in his life, he departed the bedroom unaffected. They held no sway. But she had vanquished him. He wanted to be with her and anticipated their next encounter. *Damn you, Weston Wolf, you're such a wuss. Shake it off.* But her essence remained, haunting him.

To reorient his thoughts, he focused on meeting with Underdonk. The goal was clear: take control of all aspects of the sale and somehow mediate or negotiate the highest payoff. If he could push the winning bid to twenty million dollars, he would be set for life. *Fifteen percent of twenty million is . . . uh . . . uh . . . three million dollars! Clutch your pearls, Aunt Beryl, and give them a twirl. Three million dollars!* He needed to think clearly. The key was Bacon. What did Underdonk know about his rival? Could Bacon come up with the cash to raise the stakes? How far could he push him? The worst that could happen was for one of them to drop out. Then he and Virginia would be at the other's mercy. Five million would probably be the most they could get, and that's if they were lucky. Virginia had wanted the sure thing from Bacon. Wolf peered at the ceiling as if he could see through to the sky. *Thank you, dearly departed Brother Fregiotto for bringing Underdonk into the mix.* He chuckled. *Without you I'd be trailing some banker to get a snapshot of him and his mistress doing the Devil's Tango.* He rolled over, shifted his legs off the edge of the bed and sat up. *Don't fail me, Gatsby Cap Boy. I need that meeting with Bacon.*

He put on some java, showered, dressed and gobbled down a quick bowl of corn flakes with a sliced banana. His favorite coffee cup, the insulated one with the screw-on lid, sat in the sink amidst a collection of plates, glasses and silverware. He unscrewed the lid, rinsed it out with cold water, filled it almost to the brim and dumped in a rough measure of powdered creamer. He stirred it, took a quick sip and screwed on the cap.

Back in the bedroom he glanced at his holster slung over the bedpost. *No gun, thanks to Walton and his misdirected investigation.* Undoubtedly, Wolf knew he played a major role in that misdirection. He opened his closet and dropped to his knees. After removing all the shoes, he pulled back the carpeting. A rectangular piece of plywood, about sixteen inches by twelve inches, fit snugly into a hole in the middle of the closet floor. Wolf used the tips of his fingers to grip the edge of the cutout and lift it toward him. He set the wood to the side and peered into the hidden box he had fashioned between the floor joists. Sticking his hand into the coffer, he fumbled among the bevy of handguns for the Sig Sauer semi-automatic pistol. "Ah . . . there you are — an identical twin," he said aloud as if the gun could hear him.

He replaced the wood cutout and rolled back the carpet. After getting to his feet, he kicked the shoes back into the closet and shut the door. The morning sun blazed through the window, and the surf roared and swooshed along the shoreline. He walked to the window, leaned on the ledge and took a deep breath of the fresh ocean air. *Another dazzling day on the Outer Banks.* It didn't take long to strap the holster over his t-shirt and funnel into a loose-fitting black golf shirt with its white shark logo. He checked his watch — 9:55. *The day is young, but there's a lot to do.*

Angie sat in front of her computer in the outer office, scrolling through images of vehicles. When he placed a cup of black coffee next to her, she didn't give it much more than a quick glance. "Thanks. I needed a cup."

"What are you up to, Angel? Checking out porn sites again?"

"Car porn."

She collapsed the window on the screen and faced him. "What's up?"

"A new day."

She checked her watch. "It's about time you got this day started."

"I had a late night."

"No kidding. Miss Dare didn't get back to my house until two in the morning. I almost called you to make sure everything was okay. You're lucky I didn't. I realized how distracting a phone call can be when you're in the middle of an intense tumbling session."

Wolf raised his thick eyebrows. "We were tumbling ideas and possibilities concerning the circumstances of Miss Dare's . . . predicament."

Angie angled her head a few degrees and slightly closed one eye. "I don't even want to know about last night's predicament."

Wolf offered an impish smile. "That's probably best. Enough about last night's proceedings. What's happening today? Anything new?"

She raised a finger. "Yes indeed. A young man dropped in to see you about an hour ago. I told him you were sleeping."

"What'd he look like?"

"He was about five feet ten inches tall, acne-scarred face, and wore one of those Ben Hogan golf hats, you know, the kind that young, strapping pro wears. What's his name? DeChambeau?"

"Ah yes . . . Willard Bacon. Did he say what he wanted?"

She lifted an envelope from the corner of her desk. "He left this for you."

Wolf set his coffee cup on her desk and snatched the envelope, quickly ripped the flap open and read the message. "Excellent. The game is afoot, and I'm on the hunt. I'll be meeting with Alfred Bacon this afternoon at three, but don't let anybody know about it."

Her lips knitted together, and she drew her finger across the seam.

He slipped the message into his pants pocket. "I've got a bonus question for you, a test of your observational skills. What kind of car was Gatsby Boy driving?"

She swiveled back to her computer screen and clicked on the internet icon to reopen the frame. "There," she said as she pointed to a silver car. "A 2020 Buick Cascada Premier."

Wolf bobbed his head slowly. "You are a star pupil, Angel. You keep this up, buttercup, and we'll see how you're promotion winds up."

She screwed up her face. "Did anyone ever tell you your rhyming schemes are irritating?"

"Fascinating, illuminating and invigorating but never irritating." He lifted the insulated cup from her desk and took a drink. "One more thing before I go." He sat the cup back down and pulled out his wallet, extracted Underdonk's card and handed it to her. "Call that number and tell Mr. Underdonk that I'd like to meet with him in about twenty minutes."

She dialed the number and sat with the phone pressed against her ear. After several seconds she said, "Mr. Underdonk? . . . This is Angie Stallone calling from Wolf and Stallone Detective Agency. Mr. Wolf would like to meet with you in about twenty minutes." With a wry smile, she glanced up at Wolf and asked, "Do you insist?"

"I insist. Tell him I'll come to his place." He pointed his finger at her. "And don't jump the gun on your promotion."

She smirked and put the phone back to her ear. "Yes, sir, he insists . . . at your place . . . I'll tell him . . . Third level . . . suite number 3—Beatrice Estelle . . . Got it . . . Goodbye." She hung up the phone. "He said he'll be waiting with bated breath and bells on."

Wolf tapped his temple. "Now that's a disturbing image. One more thing, Angel. Keep your eye out for that silver Cascada. Willard Bacon is a disturbed individual. I think he killed Fregiotto."

Angie took an invisible pencil and wrote across the palm of her left hand. "Got it, Mr. Boss Man."

Underdonk was staying in Manteo at the Burrus House Inn, an elegant, waterfront hotel on Shallowbag Bay. Wolf's trips over to Roanoke Island were adding up. Every time he crossed the Washington Baum Bridge the odd sense increased that *his* hand was directing the shady actors on this historical stage where America's greatest mystery began and would soon end. He made a right turn off Highway 64 just past a McDonald's onto a gravel access road. The hotel didn't fit the usual mold of franchise hotel architecture. It was s striking place with varied levels and surface textures, multiple decks and gables. *Now this is what I call boss accommodations and look at that view of the bay. Underdonk goes first class, no doubt about that.* He parked the Cougar under a huge deck next to Underdonk's Jaguar. The steps were located under the deck not far from where he parked. *Third level, suite number 3 called Beatrice Estelle. I wonder if he'll be wearing his purple Brooks Brothers suit. Wouldn't surprise me.*

Wolf hustled up the three flights of wooden steps and made his way across the deck to a large sliding glass door. He peeked in and saw Underdonk sitting in a comfortable brown leather chair with his hands interlaced and resting on his paunch. He was staring at a big screen TV mounted above a red gas log stove. Wolf rapped hard on the glass, and the little man started like spooked skunk. After taking several calming breaths, Underdonk rose from the chair, crossed the room and slid the door open.

Wearing a lavender dress shirt with ruffles and white deck pants, he bowed and swooped his arm like a ringmaster introducing a circus act. "Welcome to my humble lodging. Please come in."

Wolf stepped in and noticed a small kitchenette with a sink and microwave oven to his left. Below the black marble countertop sat a pintsize refrigerator and white cabinets. A wide doorway next to the kitchenette exposed the bedroom. A king-size bed with an elaborately carved headboard and footboard occupied the middle of the room. Looking to his right, He took in the spacious living room with its white wainscoting and high-end furniture. "Nice digs."

"They are satisfactory." Underdonk crossed the room and lifted the remote from the arm of the leather chair. Some show about shopping for an exotic beach house was playing on one of those home fix-up networks. The screen went black, and the audio cut out. He settled into the brown leather chair and motioned toward the white couch. "Have a seat."

Wolf sat down on the couch between two fluffy white pillows. "I don't see any bells on," Wolf sneered.

Underdonk patted his chest. "Bells are ringing in my heart in hopes of good news from you. Has Miss Dare made her decision?"

"Yes. She has decided to leave that decision up to me."

He rubbed his hands together as if he were applying a topical cream. "And, of course, you want me in on the sale to increase your profits."

"I haven't decided yet."

"Why not? I could double your payoff."

"Perhaps, but I don't know if I can trust you."

He lowered his arms to the armrests. "What I have I done to merit your mistrust."

"You tried to rob me."

A nervous snicker escaped his throat, sounding like a sputtering hiss. "I . . . I explained to you that my actions were based on the fact that the diary belongs to the one who possesses it. I merely tried to possess it. You must admit that Thomas Ellis sent Frank Fregiotto to steal it from some unsuspecting family."

"I don't see it that way."

"But the law does. The buyer becomes the owner of whatever is left behind in the house. Besides that, Thomas Ellis wasn't the one who originally left the diary behind. So he has no grounds on which to stand."

Wolf raised a finger. "He and Virginia are direct descendants. The law may not recognize that fact, but the blood in their veins is proof enough for me. If you can't acknowledge that truth, then you are excluded from the auction."

Underdonk sat quietly for more than a few seconds. He took a deep breath and let it out with an audible rasp. "I see your point. Blood can be a higher standard of ownership than the letter of the law."

"I'm glad you're beginning to see the light. Now you must convince me that win or lose, you will not divulge the means by which Thomas Ellis acquired the diary."

He sat straight up. "That would be imbecilic of me."

"Why?"

"Because my assent to take part in the auction would be an admission of my intention to purchase a stolen item."

"That's true unless you claim you didn't know it was stolen. But I know it was and would testify against you. That's why, whether you win the bid or not, you must never link Virginia or her father to the sale. Any questions about the chain of possessorship must be answered with the explanation that the sellers chose to remain anonymous."

"I agree. That line of response would be beneficial to both them and me."

Wolf clasped his hands behind his head and sat back. "Very good. We're beginning to understand each other. Now to the next item of importance. What did you tell Sheriff Walton when he took you in for questioning last night?"

Underdonk's eyes widened. "I said nothing that would jeopardize the parties involved in this sale. I kept my mouth shut."

"What did he ask you? How did you answer his questions?"

"He asked me how I knew Frank Fregiotto. I told him that I had purchased antiques from the store where Frank worked. We had formed a buyer—seller relationship. He asked me why we were on the Outer Banks at the same time. I simply explained that many people I know vacation on the Outer Banks this time of year. It's not unusual to run into acquaintances down here."

Wolf bobbed his head. "That sounds reasonable. What else?"

"He asked me if I hired you to do some investigative work for me. I had to think fast. I told him that I hired you to investigate a seller whom I suspected of fraud. I had purchased several rare duck decoys down here worth thousands of dollars and discovered they were counterfeit. You were checking into it for me."

"Did he go for that?"

Underdonk shrugged. "I don't know. He pressed me on it, but I stuck to the story."

"Did he ask about Virginia?"

"Yes. I told him that she and I had recently met through a mutual friendship with you. I explained that she had a terrible temper, which I unfortunately discovered over a game of charades." He lowered his eyebrows. "That's the ridiculous story you told, and I stuck with it."

"Did he believe you?"

"Of course not. He prodded and prodded me about her, Frank and you, but I remained steadfast. After several hours he gave up."

"I hope you're telling me the truth."

"I have no reason to lie."

Wolf leaned forward, elbows on his knees. "If Walton approaches me any time before the sale and tells me any compromising revelation that he learned through your interrogation. . ." He thumbed over his shoulder. ". . . then you're out."

Underdonk's features stiffened. "I'm not worried. I promise you I did not compromise our enterprise."

"We'll see. Now to my next avenue of inquiry — Alfred Bacon."

"What about him?"

"How well do you know him?"

"Being in the antiquities business for many years, we have crossed paths. At times we've competed for the same objects at auctions. I usually win."

"Because you have a fatter wallet?"

"Yes. I have been very successful at buying and selling rare objects."

Wolf crossed his ankles and rubbed his chin. "The Dare Diary could offer the greatest success of your career. You may be able to sell it for thirty million or more."

He raised his eyebrows and nodded. "That's true."

"When does Bacon win?"

"Pardon?"

"When does Bacon beat you at an auction?"

"On those occasions when he comes prepared to outbid me."

"I see." Wolf bit his upper lip for a second or two. "When he wants an item bad enough, he is able to acquire the financial backing."

Underdonk nodded. "He has connections."

"Mob connections."

"Correct."

Wolf grinned like a coyote eyeing a chicken coop. "How high are you willing to go to win the diary?"

"Fifteen million. That's my limit."

Wolf stood. "That's not enough. Sorry, Mr. Underdonk, but if that's your limit, you're not in." Wolf stepped around the couch and headed for the door.

"Wait a minute." Underdonk sprang to his feet and rushed toward Wolf with choppy steps. "What do you mean? A winning bid of ten or fifteen million is a winning bid."

"We're not going to let the diary go for less than twenty million."

Underdonk's round face appeared to sag as if the force of gravity tripled. He took a wheezing breath and said, "Okay, okay. I'll come prepared to bid twenty million, but that's my limit."

"Good enough." Wolf extended his hand to the little man. "You're in." His handshake was soft and clammy. Wolf withdrew his hand and eyed his palm with trepidation as if he had just touched poison ivy. He wiped his hand on his shirt. "If you win the bid, we will go directly to the bank to make the cash transfers. Fifteen percent will go into my account. Eighty-five percent will go to Miss Dare. When we are assured of the transaction, then we will hand over the diary. Make sure you have the capital ready and available."

Underdonk rubbed his hand across his forehead, over his left eye and down his cheek. "You've got me clinging to a cliff, and you're holding the rope, Mr. Wolf. I'll make sure my finances are in order."

"Good. The sale will take place tomorrow. I'll let you know when and where. One last thing. What really happened to Robert Ellis? The police say suicide, you claim it was an accident, and Miss Dare believes you killed him. What's the truth?"

Underdonk frowned, his eyes watering. "All of the above. That's all I'm going to say about it."

Wolf stood silently for several seconds, turned, slid open the door and left.

Chapter 13

Wolf decided to stop by Angie's place to see Virginia. Was he infatuated with her? Addicted to being near her? Maybe. More importantly, he needed to update her on the situation and find out when and where her father would deliver the diary. Angie lived in a modest two-bedroom ranch-style home along Barracuda Road just north of Nags Head Golf Links. The neighborhood consisted mostly of fulltime residents who earned a living fishing or working in the tourist industry and managing local shops. These were the people who kept the Outer Banks going in the late fall and winter months when the barrier islands emptied out and money got tight. They endured hurricanes, economic hardship and isolation during the off season but would never trade their lives for the comforts and security that inlanders held dear. Living on the edge of the ocean was risky but invigorating.

Wolf pulled into her driveway and parked near the front steps which led up to a redwood deck. Angie had created a welcoming flower bed using paving stones near the bottom of the steps. About six-foot square, the area bloomed with bright red and pink hibiscus blossoms. The house had white siding and green shutters, somewhat weatherworn but well kept. Wolf climbed the few steps, opened the screen and rapped on the door.

The curtain of the window to his right lifted, and someone peeked through the narrow gap. Wolf waved. The door opened, and Virginia faced him wearing white shorts and a blue-striped button down top. Her long white legs, well-shaped but not muscular, seemed to go on forever. Wolf smiled and said, "How's life on the sound side of the island?"

"I'm so glad you're here." She stretched and yawned. "I'm bored to death sitting around, drinking coffee and watching morning talk shows. Let's do something."

"How about some lunch?"

"Perfect. I'm famished. Step inside and give me a few minutes to get ready."

When Wolf entered, she slipped her hands around his waist and embraced him tightly. She lifted her head and said, "Give me a kiss. I didn't get enough of you last night." He cupped the back of her head and kissed her, a soft wet kiss that lasted almost a minute. She stepped back and said, "Whew! Don't get me started. Be back in a minute." She turned and hurried through a doorway that led down a hall.

Wolf glanced around the room. The furniture was somewhat threadbare but neatly ordered: a green plaid couch, a scuffed yellow rocking chair with green cushions, a faux leather recliner, and a midsized flat screen TV mounted on the far wall. The oak coffee table in front of the couch was littered with police magazines — *Police Journal, Inside Detective, The Police Marksmen.* Wolf shook his head and smiled. *The girl is definitely obsessed with learning the trade.*

Virginia entered the room with a wide smile. "Let's go before I black out from hunger."

Wolf drove to the Blue Moon Beach Grill less than a mile away along Route 158. The place had great lunch specials including Wolf's favorite, the Beach Burger, a third pound of prime angus loaded with extras like mushrooms, onions, bacon and tomatoes. His mouth was watering as he pulled into the parking lot. A yellow sign mounted on the roof announced "Welcome to the Moon" in dark blue letters. They entered, and the hostess led them to a table on the far right against a cobalt blue wall. An impressive oil painting of crashing waves and a blustery sky hung above the table. A plump redheaded waitress wearing a dark blue top with the restaurant's circular logo took their orders. Wolf wanted the

Beach Burger and fries. Virginia gave him a disapproving glance and opted for the spinach and arugula salad. They both ordered beers, Yuengling lagers. The waitress whirled and hurried away.

"So what's happening in your world?" she asked.

"I've been working hard for you."

"How so?"

"I met with Underdonk today. Needed to make sure that he kept his mouth shut."

"Did he?"

"Said he did. We'll see. If Sheriff Walton comes looking for you, we'll know he tattled."

"That would be disastrous."

"Keep your fingers crossed. I also asked him how much he was willing to bid on the diary. He said he'd go up to fifteen million."

Her dark eyes widened. "That's good!"

Wolf shook his head. "No, it's not. I told him we wouldn't let the diary go for less than twenty. Then I headed for the door."

"Are you crazy?"

Wolf grinned. "Like a poker player holding a royal flush. He came after me faster than a fat kid chasing an ice cream truck. Said he'd meet my demands."

Virginia clasped her hands in front of her on the table. "I'm impressed. You're good at what you do . . . both as a lover and a detective."

Wolf wondered if she loved him. He hoped she did. He wasn't good at reading women, especially hard-edged ones who make a habit of lying. "I try."

"You more than try. You know how to please." She smiled coyly.

"I'm meeting with Bacon this afternoon."

"Please don't make him mad."

"Why? I'm not afraid of him."

"I am. He expected to do the deal for five million. When he gets angry, bad things happen. Twenty million will make him go psycho. I don't think he can come up with that much money."

Wolf took a long drink from his bottle of beer. "Oh yes, he can. Underdonk told me he has connections to the mob. When he wants something, he gets it."

She clamped her hands to the sides of her head. "The mob? Now the mob is going to get involved in this?"

"I don't care whose pockets he dips into. That diary is a gold mine for whoever wins the bid. He'll make it back double or triple."

She raked her fingers through her hair and said, "I hope you know what you're doing."

"You just keep hiding out at Angie's and let me handle everything. First we need to determine where the sale will take place."

"I was considering that, perhaps the back room of a local restaurant."

"That's a possibility, although a public facility is not ideal — too many variables beyond our control. Both Underdonk and Bacon are staying at hotels on Roanoke Island near the waterfront. Either one of their places could provide the privacy we need."

"That's fine. You decide."

"I'll check out Bacon's suite this afternoon and consider the options." Wolf rubbed his chin and panned the restaurant, trying to remember what other details he needed to clear up. He noticed a wooden surfboard with three fins on the back hanging above the wide window between the kitchen and serving area. The image clicked his memory. "Ah yes, another thing of great importance: I need to know where and when the diary is going to arrive."

She leaned closer and spoke lowly. "My father messaged me this morning. Everything is set. He's delivering the diary himself by boat tomorrow afternoon. He'll text me fifteen minutes before he arrives. He doesn't want the exact details known until then. Father is always thinking two steps ahead."

Wolf nodded slowly. "Your dad is a shrewd man. I'm looking forward to meeting him."

She smiled, a slight blush reddening her face. "He has a flair for the dramatic. I wanted to make the sale in Charlotte, but he insisted that the transaction be made on the same island where Eleanor began writing the diary. He sent me ahead to give him time to prepare."

"Clearly, he appreciates the historical significance of the sale. That's one of many reasons I'm here today. If you would have made the transaction in Charlotte, we would have never met. The randomness of life has aligned all my ducks perfectly."

She twisted her mouth slightly to the side and raised an eyebrow. "I'd say fate has brought you to this table."

Wolf turned to see the waitress approaching with their meals. "Here comes our food."

The redhead placed his plate loaded with the huge burger and pile of fries in front of him. Then she pivoted and delivered Virginia's salad.

Wolf noticed her nametag. "Beverly, can I ask you a question?"

She placed her hands on her wide hips. "Sure thing, Hon."

"Did this Beach Burger arrive here by fate or the randomness of life?"

She smiled and tilted her head. "Lemme think about that . . . I'd say the cow was picked randomly, but the poor critter couldn't escape its fate—the slaughterhouse."

Wolf laughed. "Good answer."

The meal was delicious. Wolf gobbled it down, sat back and stretched his arms above his head.

Virginia glared at him. "You eat like your namesake — a starved wolf. I'm only halfway done."

Wolf grinned and motioned to the waitress to get the check. He noticed Deputy Joel Thomas standing at the entrance near the cash register. Deputy Thomas waved, strolled in their direction and stopped beside their table.

"Hey, Wes, we seem to be crossing paths all the time nowadays." He was wearing his gray uniform and black ballcap with the Hatteras Lighthouse logo.

"That's pretty random, huh?" Wolf asked.

"Sometimes."

Wolf motioned toward Virginia. "Do you remember my girlfriend, Emma Ritz?"

"Sure." Deputy Thomas tipped his hat. "How could I forget? You're the first person I ever saw thump someone with a cane over a game of charades."

Virginia raised her beer and offered a farcical smile. "I take my charades seriously."

"How'd the interrogation go with my client?" Wolf asked.

"Not so good. Underdonk didn't give us much of anything to help."

"No clues? No persons of interest?

"Nope."

"Too bad." Wolf eyed Virginia and noticed tension fade from her face.

"Yeah. We were hoping to get a break, but this case is truly a puzzle: two bodies found within a quarter mile of each other, both gunshot victims."

Wolf crossed his arms. "Am I still a prime suspect in both murders?"

"Sheriff Walton thinks you are, but I don't."

Wolf uncrossed his arms and pointed at him. "You're a smart man. How about my gun? When do I get it back?"

"Tests should be back soon. I'll run it over to your office once we're done with it."

Wolf rubbed his hands together and smirked. "That's awful nice of you, Joel, but I know the real reason you want to stop by my office."

Deputy Thomas nodded, his face reddening. "I guess it's pretty obvious, huh?"

"You're a lovestruck young man."

Deputy Thomas shifted his feet back and forth. "Angie is a wonderful girl."

"Wonderful and smart, too. She wants to go into law enforcement." Wolf glanced at Virginia, winked and then eyed the deputy. "I think you two would make a good pair."

A wide smile broke across his clean-shaven face. "I truly appreciate your blessing."

"Make sure you treat her right."

His eyes tensed with sincerity. "You can count on me, Wes."

"I know I can count on you. It's too bad Sheriff Walton is such a hardhead. If he would treat me right, I could help him solve these murders. By late tomorrow afternoon, I could wrap this case up, put a ribbon around it and bow on top."

Deputy Thomas lowered his head. "Are you serious, Wes?"

"I'm just saying."

"We think we know who killed your partner. Had to be Fregiotto. We just can't prove it. Do you know who killed Fregiotto?"

"I have a good idea."

Deputy Thomas straightened and placed his hands on his hips. "Who?"

"I don't want to say yet. Ask me tomorrow afternoon."

"If you did help us solve this case, I bet Sheriff Walton would be impressed."

Wolf shut one eye nearly closed. "I wouldn't go that far, Joel. I'd have to walk across Shallowbag Bay, delivering irrefutable evidence and a pepperoni pizza to impress Walton."

Chapter 14

After dropping Virginia off at Angie's, Wolf headed to the office to check on things. Angie was typing away on the keyboard and barely noticed when he entered. She stopped, leaned nearer the computer screen and read what she had written, silently mouthing the words. "That sounds good," she said.

"Are you writing to Dear Abby?"

She glanced over her shoulder and eyed him with a peeved look. "Not hardly. I'm finishing up a paper on the underlying causes of criminal behavior."

"Interesting." Wolf meandered over to her desk. "Do you know what the Russians believe to be the main cause of criminal behavior?"

"The Russians?"

"Yeah, you know, communist Russia."

She took a frustrated breath and blew it out. "I give up."

"Capitalism."

"No kidding."

"The desire for wealth in a system based on private ownership and a free market adds up to one thing."

Angie swiveled her chair toward him. "And what's that?"

"Greed."

"Are you a capitalist?"

Wolf fluttered his eyebrows, Groucho Marx style. "Yes, indeed."

"Sometimes I worry about you, Mr. Boss Man. For a guy dedicated to righting wrongs, knowing good from evil and standing up for the underdog, you sure spend a lot of time in the gray areas of life."

"I hate to break the news to you, Angel, but the gray area is where life happens."

Angie scooted back to her desk and stared at the screen. "Thanks for the life lesson."

"I won't charge you for that one. Besides, you shouldn't worry about me. Most of the time I do the right thing."

Angie laughed. "Most of the time . . . depending on the circumstances."

"Anything happen here today that I should know about?"

Angie swiveled toward him again, her face losing all its humor. "Yes. I almost forgot. Your old flame stopped in to see you — Laura Bain."

Wolf clamped his hands onto the sides of his head, his hair springing in between his fingers. "Nooooo!"

"She said that she's sorry for everything and wants to see you soon to make up for what she did."

He stomped his foot. "You've got to be kidding? She tells me she wants to see me burn in hell, tells the cops I murdered her husband, and now she wants to make up with me? She can't have it both ways."

Angie raised a finger. "Perhaps you could give her a life lesson."

"I plan on it. Next time she shows up, tell her I don't want to see her anymore and to stay the hell away from me and this office."

She patted her chest. "You want me to tell her? I guess I'm your teaching assistant."

Wolf gave her a doubletake. "Here's another life lesson for you, Angel: Whatever you do, don't get mixed up with somebody who doesn't know the North Pole from the South Pole. You'll soon discover that person is bipolar."

"Don't worry about me. I'm dating a guy who's very levelheaded."

Wolf clapped his hands. "That reminds me. I ran into your boyfriend today over at the Blue Moon Beach Grill. I told him I gave my full approval of your relationship. Soon he will be proposing marriage."

Angie gave him a mock smile. "You're so omniscient where my life is concerned. Thank you so much for your endorsement."

"You're welcome." Wolf walked to his office door but hesitated and turned around. "And don't use big words like omniscient, or I won't know what you're talking about."

Angie waved him away. "That's the point."

Driving over the Washington Baum Bridge to Roanoke Island, Wolf considered the legalities of his circumstances. His talk with Angie had struck a nerve on the exposed surface of his conscience. He hated when that happened. *I didn't steal the diary. Besides, shouldn't the old journal belong to the direct descendants? Virginia has proven that she's Eleanor Dare's offspring through the DNA analysis. I'm only an agent in this transaction. I've been hired to do a job. That's all. I can't control what happened before I arrived on the scene. I can only do what I've been hired to do. And then, of course, collect my fifteen percent.*

He glanced at the note Willard Bacon had dropped off at the office, which sat on the compartment divider between the front seats. *Cameron House Inn, 300 Budleigh Street. Sandpiper Room located behind the inn in the annex building.* Wolf chuckled to himself. The Cameron House Inn was a quaint bed and breakfast, but Bacon wanted more isolation than one of the rooms in the main house offered. The annex building checked off the privacy box. Turning off Highway 64, he drove onto Budleigh Street, slowing the Cougar to under twenty miles an hour. He checked out the houses as he passed. Unlike the beach houses along the outer islands with their thick posts raising them ten feet off the ground, the Manteo homes resembled good ol' small-town America. Most of them had white or gray siding and gable roofs. Every so often a redbrick residence stood out here or there amongst them. After a couple of blocks, Wolf caught sight of the red Cameron House Inn sign mounted on a wooden post. He pulled into an empty parking space along the street behind a sleek gray Rolls Royce Phantom Drophead Coupe. Beyond it he saw the silver Cascada. *Uncle Alfred and his nephew have great tastes in automobiles. I'll say that much for them.*

Wolf climbed out of the Cougar and flung the door shut with a loud clonk. The front of the inn was unique with its entry pergola that led to the wide porch. Vines had climbed up the front posts of the pergola and stretched across the wooden horizontal beams, giving the entry an exotic look. The house itself was an Arts and Crafts bungalow, a popular style a hundred years ago when these types of homes on the island were built. The owners had done an excellent job of restoring the building to its original luster. White wooden shingles brightly covered the exterior. The porch, painted slate-gray, welcomed visitors with a couple wooden rockers and a white porch swing, cushioned and loaded with brown pillows. Lush green plants were stationed on each side of the black front door. Just above the porch, a dormer peeked out from the middle of the hipped roof.

Remembering the Sandpiper Room was located in the annex building, Wolf angled toward the side of the house and headed for the back. He noticed a breezeway that cut through the annex building, so he turned toward the opening and took two quick steps onto the wooden decking. His heart jumped when he saw Willard Bacon leaning against the wall and smoking a cigarette in the shadows. He wore faded jeans, a brown button-down shirt and his familiar Gatsby cap. The smoke encircled his head like a ghost snake.

Wolf quickly collected himself. "Willard Bacon, it's good to see you again. It's been too long." His tone exhibited an obvious counterfeit good-naturedness.

Willard dropped his cigarette and crushed it with his oiled-leather boot. He raised his head and said, "Scared you shitless, didn't I?"

Wolf grinned. "You're a helluva scary fellow."

"Keep it up, Asswipe, and I just might scare you to death." He leaned his head toward a door, reached and opened it. "This way."

Wolf entered and climbed winding carpeted steps to a second-floor suite. He passed a bathroom with its black and white chessboard floor and updated fixtures. Then came a walled nook like an open closet with a dresser and a mirror above it. A couple bottles of booze and whiskey glasses sat on the dresser next to an ice bucket. The suite opened into a spacious bedroom with two lavishly made queen beds. Their thick oak headboards and footboards stood on ball feet with finials on the corners.

The deep purples and greens of the walls gave the place a classy touch. A large man sat in a brown wicker chair against the far wall next to the window. Wolf noticed a matching wicker chair to his left next to an old-fashioned desk. An antique bronze lamp in the middle of the desk shed its light on the immaculately restored maple surface, and a newspaper lay folded next to the lamp.

The large man had black hair streaked with gray strands and combed over from a part that started halfway down the side of his head. Thick, dark eyebrows flourished above dark brown eyes that bulged slightly, creating shadows and creases under the lids. His wide, flat nose matched his broad face. Thick lips failed to completely cover his front teeth, which were somewhat crooked with gaps between each. He wore a gray Nike sweat outfit and looked like an old defensive tackle, who hadn't exercised in years but could still execute a good horse collar on an unsuspecting running back.

Wolf nodded at the man. "Mr. Bacon, I presume. My name's Weston Wolf."

Bacon took a raspy breath and said, "You must be the private dick that wants to run this show." His voice sounded like he just ate a gravel sandwich.

Wolf swallowed. "I wouldn't put it exactly that way."

His head moved slightly, and his eyes bore into Wolf. "How would you put it?"

"Miss Dare hired me to manage the sale."

"I see. You're a sales manager like one of those middle-aged broads who work at Walmart."

Wolf smiled. "If you want the blue-light special, you've got to come through me."

"Have a seat, Mr. Blue-light Special."

Wolf sat down on the wicker chair beside the desk and glanced around the room. "I like the place. It has that roaring twenties feel to it."

"Let's make it authentic. How about a drink?"

Wolf shrugged. "I'm on the job, but what the hell. I'm self-employed."

"Yeah," Bacon grunted, "what the hell. Rum or whiskey?"

"Rum."

"Willard, fix Mr. Blue-Light and me a couple glasses of rum."

Wolf heard Gatsby Boy fumbling with glasses and ice behind him near the dresser. "That's some employee you got there, Mr. Bacon. I caught him sleeping on the job yesterday."

Bacon frowned. "What do you mean?"

Willard came through and handed a glass of rum to Wolf, crossed the room and handed the other glass to Bacon. Then he sat on the bed facing the window and slid a cigarette out of his front shirt pocket.

Wolf took a sip. "Not bad." He waved toward Willard. "Like I was saying, I caught him sleeping in his car when he was supposed to be keeping his eye on me."

Bacon shifted in his chair and glared at Willard. "Is that true?"

Willard fumbled with his cigarette, and it fell on the floor. He picked it up, stuck it in his mouth and shrugged. "I was taking a catnap." The cigarette flipped as he talked. "Blue-Light Boy took forever in that bookstore."

Bacon shook his head. "You dumb jackass. I ought to swat that kisser of yours until you bleed like a two-bit boxer."

Willard sat up straight and expanded his chest, the cigarette dipping down to his chin. His facial muscles tightened, and his lips quivered, but he kept his mouth shut. Finally, he said, "I need to light up and smoke."

"Not in here!" Bacon growled. "Go outside. I don't want to look at that ugly crater face of yours for the next half hour."

Willard rose and stomped out of the room and down the steps.

Wolf grimaced. "You've got to watch hiring relatives. Sometimes they take advantage of the blood ties."

"Hmmph." Bacon took a swig of rum. "Willard does what I tell him to do most of the time."

"I've seen his handiwork up close. So did Frank Fregiotto."

A malicious grin darkened Bacon's face. "Poor Frank has departed this island for distant shores. Too bad he didn't abide by the rules of the game."

"I heard he tried to up the ante. Is that why you ordered Willard to kill him?"

The grin faded. "What do I look like? Some sap that you can hang a murder rap on? I gave no such orders, and Willard didn't kill anybody. I'd say you're the logical suspect. Didn't Fregiotto kill your partner? Revenge—that's the only motive that makes sense to me."

Wolf shook his head. "I wouldn't say the motive was revenge. His murder was simply a penalty to be paid for breaking your rules."

Bacon cleared his throat. "We'll have to agree to disagree on that issue. Let's talk about the sale."

"Let's."

"I made a solid deal with Virginia Dare, and I expect that deal to be concluded."

"Don't get your hopes up."

Bacon leaned forward on his knees and lowered his eyebrows. "Why not?"

"You made a lowball offer. Underdonk is going to easily double it."

Bacon straightened. "Five million dollars is not a lowball offer."

"C'mon, Mr. Bacon. You know the reality of the situation. The Dare Diary is one of the most important documental finds in American history. Whoever purchases it from us will double or triple their money in a matter of months. There's no way I will let it be sold for less than twenty million."

"Twenty million? Who's got twenty million?"

"Mr. Underdonk is willing to go that high, and I know you have connections."

Bacon pointed a thick finger at Wolf. "This is my deal, not Underdonk's. If you insist on bringing in Underdonk and inflating the price, you better watch your back. A contract is a contract."

Wolf sprang to his feet, knocking the chair backward. "You listen to me, you old fat bastard! You're either in this auction or you're out. You're not dealing with some smalltime chiseler like Frank Fregiotto. You're dealing with me."

Bacon rose to his feet and shook his fist. "The hell with you!"

"The hell with you!" Wolf spun and walked toward the steps. He skidded to a stop, whipped around and said, "And another thing I forgot to mention. If you want out of this deal, that's fine, but when I caught your hatchet man napping yesterday, I took his gun away from him. If you don't believe me, ask him. That gun is in a secure place with detailed instructions for the Dare County Sheriff's Department in the case of my untimely demise. You know what they say about revenge: Guns forget, but bullets don't." Wolf pulled his wallet from his back pocket, slipped out a business card and tossed it on the floor. "My cell number is on that card. You've got two hours to make a decision." He pivoted, trotted down the stairs and out the door onto the breezeway.

Gatsby Boy sat on the steps, smoking. "See ya, Blue-Light Boy," he said as Wolf passed.

Wolf stopped and glared at him. "I'll see you behind bars unless your boss decides to play nice."

Willard blew out a stream of smoke, his eyes squinting as if the words were acid sprayed at his face.

Chapter 15

As Wolf pulled away from the curb, he felt an odd sensation in the pit of his stomach. He expected a contentious meeting with Alfred Bacon. That wasn't the problem. Something felt off. Was he making a mistake? Was he building a house of cards that would come crashing down on him? The legal issues bothered him more than anything else. Yes, there was money to be made, lots of it. He'd already dipped his hand into the till. But did the opportunity to reap a big profit blind him to the consequences of orchestrating a questionable deal? He needed to talk to his attorney again before he got so tangled up in this mess that he couldn't figure a way out. After crossing the Washington Baum Bridge, he turned left up Croatan Highway and headed for Kill Devil Hills.

Jeremy House would be surprised to see him. He had just been there two days ago checking on detective—client privileges. Fortunately, House didn't charge him for these consultations. Wolf always termed them as friendly visits. House called them charity work for a freeloading private eye. Of course, whenever House needed any kind of investigation done, Wolf was happy to oblige pro bono.

He entered the office and waved at Kelly, the blonde secretary. "Hey, Gorgeous, are you still working for this ambulance chaser?"

She halted her typing and peered at him through oversized, pink-framed eyeglasses. "C'mon now, Wes, Jeremy doesn't chase ambulances. He's too busy getting guys like you out of trouble." She wore a pink blouse fastened at the top with an oval cameo. Through the glass-topped desk he noticed her black midi dress which managed to cover the tops her knees.

"Thanks for reminding me. That's exactly why I'm here."

"Trouble again, huh?"

"I can't seem to help it. I need to settle down, marry a gal like you and steer clear of the world's hornets' nests."

"That's not going to happen. You've got a better chance of surviving a forest fire wearing a kerosene kilt."

Wolf raised an eyebrow. "Are you picturing me wearing a kilt? The Scots hang freely when they wear those things."

She shook her head, pressed the button on the intercom and said, "Wes Wolf is here to see you again."

"Tell him I'm busy reviewing important documents and to come back next week," came the fuzzy reply.

She smiled and nodded toward the frosted door. "Go right in."

Wolf entered the office and slumped into the padded armchair across from House's desk. "I'm back."

"I can see that." House wore the same old crimson tie, white shirt and blue-framed reading glasses. "Let me guess. Sheriff Dugan Walton is seeking a warrant for your arrest for obstruction of justice."

Wolf sat up and nodded slowly. "Yeah. I'm sure that's true, but that's not what I'm worried about."

"Of course not." House slid off his glasses, flipped them onto the desk and interlaced his hands in front of him. "The boat's sinking, but you're worried about catching a damn fish."

Wolf spread his hands. "Not just a damn fish, a marlin bigger than the boat itself."

"What the hell have you gotten yourself into?"

Wolf settled his forearms back on the arms of the chair. "Remember the client I told you about?"

House nodded. "The one you're protecting from the investigation."

"Right."

"You said she had a once in a lifetime opportunity."

"Exactly. Not only did she hire me to protect her but also to oversee this opportunity."

House separated his hands and turned his palms up. "Okay. So far I don't see any problems."

"She has acquired a very rare and valuable item. My responsibility is to contact potential buyers, secure a locale to conduct a private sale, and deliver the item to the highest bidder."

House set his elbows on the arms of his swivel chair and bounced his fingertips off one another. "So you are the auctioneer in this transaction."

Wolf shrugged. "You could say that."

"What's the problem?"

Wolf scratched his chin. "First of all, the potential buyers are sketchy. They'd bring a bag full of tarantulas at a kid's birthday party."

House unfolded a hand toward Wolf. "That's why you were hired. You carry a gun. You are the enforcer."

Wolf patted his Sig Sauer under his black Polo shirt. "That's a fact, but they aren't the real problem."

"If it's not the buyers, then it must be the seller."

"She's a little sketchy, too, but, no, it's not her. It's the valuable object."

House leaned forward. "It's stolen?"

Wolf grimaced.

"That makes this consultation easy." He wiggled his fingers. "Let go. Step out. Say adios and go on your merry way. Let these characters slug it out. If they get caught, too bad. In fact, you should be on the other side of the fence in this situation."

"Well . . . here's the thing." Wolf itched his nose and sniffed. "I . . . I could make out big here, and the object rightfully belongs to the seller."

House circled his hand in front of him. "Explain."

"The object is a family heirloom that has been passed down for centuries. It was hidden in an old house and accidentally left there. The house was sold. But then my client remembered where it was hidden."

"That muddles things up. Usually, the buyer is granted ownership of everything that is left behind at the property."

Wolf bobbed his head. "I understand that, but this heirloom is worth millions of dollars."

"Millions?"

Wolf nodded. "It wouldn't be fair for my client to lose out on untold wealth to a totally unconnected family over real estate laws. Besides, I'll earn fifteen percent from the sale."

"Whoa!" House pulled a pen out of his shirt pocket and tapped it on the desk. "Can she prove rightful ownership through a chain of provenance?"

"The heirloom can be identified as belonging to a certain colonial family, and my client has proven through a DNA analysis that she is a direct descendant of this family."

House closed his eyes and wobbled his head. "That's a step in the right direction, but the waters are still murky. She may not be the only descendant. Do the owners of the house know this item was stolen?"

"No. They believe another object of great value was stolen, and they have been compensated. However, when the heirloom is resold publicly, there's an outside chance they may suspect something."

"That's not good. Someone pulled a fast one on them." House inserted the pen back into his pocket. "Man, you have flown into a cloud bank. Legally this is a gray area. Slate gray."

"That's why I'm here."

House took a deep breath and blew it out the side of his mouth. "I need more time. There may be some precedents that would clarify your position. We're talking hours of research. I may have to charge you."

"That's fine. I'd feel better knowing I'm on solid ground. Can you let me know by tonight?"

"Tonight! This could take several days." House spread his hands above his desk. "And I've got important work sitting right here in front of me."

Wolf hung his head. "Crap. I don't have several days."

"Sorry, buddy. There's no way I can give you a sound answer by tonight."

Wolf smiled weakly. "Figures. I'll just have to fly blind into that cloud bank."

Wolf checked his watch—4:20. An hour had passed since he'd left the Cameron House Inn, and Bacon still hadn't called. Instead of heading back to the office, he turned west onto Route 64 and headed across the Washington Baum Bridge again to Roanoke Island. His talk with Jeremy House did little to clear his mental fog. He needed to walk and think. Usually, he went to Jockey's Ridge State Park when he felt perplexed and trudged through the hot sand, enduring the desert-like heat. Suffering cleared his mind and gave him a sense of penance. Now he felt drawn to the north end of Roanoke Island where the Fort Raleigh Historic Site was located. He had met with Underdonk near the site the other night in the theater parking lot. For some reason he wanted to walk the paths that Thomas Ellis, Eleanor Dare and her father John White had walked.

The drive to the north end of the island took about ten minutes. He turned onto Fort Raleigh Road, drove about a quarter mile and parked near the Fort Raleigh Visitor Center. He stepped out of the car with the intention of finding a lonely path through the woods where he could clear his mind. It didn't take long to find that path at an opening near some flowering shrubs and a thicket of trees.

He walked through the shadows. The fluttering leaves above him shifted the dappled sunlight across the earthen floor. Old, gnarled live oaks creaked softly in the breeze, as if mildly complaining about the tangled vines that had enveloped them over the years. A squirrel scurried across the path and scrambled up a mulberry tree. Two blackbirds twittered and fussed not far away on a low hanging branch. His mind meshed with nature's ambience, and he walked without thinking through the cool shade for more than a hundred yards.

He stopped when he heard something clicking like a child's windup toy. Ten feet away he spotted a timber rattler in the middle of the path eyeing him. It was thick-bodied and semi-camouflaged with its tan and brown stripes. He backed up slowly. The segmented tail rattled ominously again. Glancing to his left, he saw an alternate path. He pivoted and strode quickly in the new direction. At a safe distance he stopped. His heart thumped and sweat dripped from his brow. He held out his hand, and it trembled slightly. *That was some coincidence. Never thought I'd run into a rattlesnake on the Outer Banks. 'Bout scared the crap out of me.*

The adrenaline rush triggered mental images of the last few days: Willard Bacon, standing in the shadows and smoking a cigarette; Hugh Underdonk, pointing his handgun directly at his chest; Alfred Bacon, lowering his eyebrows and glaring maliciously. He laughed to himself. I guess I have run into a few rattlesnakes lately. He continued down the path. *Was the serpent some kind of omen? Perhaps a warning about what might happen if I try to pull off this shady deal? No. I don't believe in omens, superstitions, karma or prophecies. Life just happens. Even better, I make things happen.*

That had been his motto for many years—make it happen. That's why he started his own business. *You either take control of the engine and direct your own destiny, or life grabs you by the collar and tosses you from the train. Then you end up like a wino living under some godforsaken bridge.* Nope. Wolf was not going to let that happen. He was going to take all that Hugh Underdonk or Alfred Bacon would cough up. *Man, my head hurts. I need an Advil.* His self-cheerleading session didn't seem to be working. At that moment he felt like the train was about to come off the tracks. Tomorrow he may guide that train into Payday Junction, but for now he wanted some quiet assurance.

The path led to a sandy shore lapped by the waters of the Albemarle Sound. An old dock extended into the water. It had fallen into disrepair, the posts and planks weatherworn and ragged. Wolf imagined a sixteenth century sailing vessel approaching with its three sails billowing in the wind. *This is probably where they came ashore.* A sense of history enveloped him. *They were adventurers and risk takers. Didn't they know the odds were against them?* Wolf shook his head. *The last thing they expected was to be abandoned—middleclass men, women and children ditched on a primitive island amidst hostile natives to fend for themselves. And one of the women, Eleanor Dare, was several months pregnant.*

The plight of the colonists weighed upon him. He ambled along the shore wondering if he failed to grasp the degree of risk he dared to assume. He noticed an opening that led back into the woods and entered the shadows. If the ghosts of John White, Eleanor Dare and Thomas Ellis would walk with him along these paths, what would they tell him? *Turn back before it's too late. Don't be a fool. If you step into a snake pit you're bound to get bitten.* Did they regret coming to the New World? Maybe. But then again, maybe not. Perhaps they were like him. Playing it safe wasn't an appealing option. Hell, they crossed an ocean and settled in an untamed wilderness with the hopes of a better life. If things went well, they would become the gentry class of the New World.

Of course, it didn't go well, but you've got to admire their courage. They gave it their all. A few even survived and thrived, living out their lives intermixing with the natives. One generation beget the next, and here we are. He remembered the first time Virginia Dare walked into his office with those long legs, creamy shoulders and beautiful face. She captivated him from their first encounter. *The ghosts of these woods live on in her. Literally, she carries their DNA.* Wolf chuckled to himself. *Like her long-lost relatives, she refuses to play it safe.*

No wonder he fell for her. They were a lot alike. Despite her flaws, he valued her determination to step into the engine of life's train and direct her destiny. She and her father inherited the same genes from those colonists who stepped off the boat not far from here. They felt compelled to steal the diary. Taking the risk had been wired into their DNA. Now they had the opportunity to take what they believed was their rightful inheritance and make something out of it. With the money from the sale they would become independently wealthy—just what their ancestors had hoped to be.

But will history repeat itself? Now Wolf realized what caused that sense of unease within. There were no guarantees. So many things could go wrong. If things came crashing down, what would happen to him? Arrest? Scandal? Jail time? Maybe even death? Would he lose everything and end up under some godforsaken bridge sipping on a bottle of Boone's Farm? He had worked hard to get this far in life. He had built his agency from scratch. Was he willing to bet it all on this questionable transaction? He thought about Angie Stallone and her dedication to her work and future. What would happen to her?

Stop it! I can't make my decisions based on Angie's future. She has her own life to live. This is my one big chance. Dammit. I started down this path, and I need to keep going. He stopped and listened to the sounds of the woods. Insects whirred. Birds chirped. Butterflies flitted. Small animals scampered. *These woods don't care which direction I go. The ghosts of the past aren't going to give me any answers. I'm not going to see any signs or visions out here that will show me the way. It's on me.* He shifted his focus from tree to tree, the myriad splashes of greens, yellows and browns shifting like a kaleidoscope. His head pounded. Steadying himself, he noticed a ghostly glow through the leaves. *What the hell?*

He walked toward the glow. The path, jumbled with weeds and leaves, crossed a neatly trimmed walkway. He turned onto it. Ahead he saw the white, glimmering figure of a nude woman standing on a pedestal and surrounded by pink and white flowers. *Where am I? Geesh! I've wandered into the Elizabethan Gardens.* Wolf knew of the period gardens with their Tudor gate house, brick walls, exotic and native plants, and Renaissance statues, but he had never visited them. They had been built decades ago to honor Queen Elizabeth II. Located near the outdoor theater, they had become a popular tourist attraction.

Wolf focused on the statue. The sun beamed down on the white marble, creating a ghostly radiance amidst the shadows. The figure of the nude woman had short hair and a splendid body, graceful and elegant in all its lines. Her arms crossed casually in front of her with beads circling her biceps and a strand around her neck. An exquisitely carved fishnet hung from her waist and down her backside, but her long white legs were exposed. She stood on a brown marble pedestal in front of an ancient live oak. *Who is this woman?* He drew closer and read the nameplate on the pedestal: *Virginia Dare!*

Wolf felt like he'd just stepped into the Twilight Zone. Strangely enough, the statue resembled the flesh and blood Virginia Dare. His no-nonsense attitude toward signs and omens threatened to crumble like an old stone building in an earthquake. He stared at the glowing face. She gazed off into the distance, motionless, as if seeing the future. That's it! Virginia Dare was the answer. He had been drawn to her from the first just like he had been drawn to this statue out of the dark woods. She saw a future of great prosperity and freedom, but she needed his help to achieve it. Together they would make it happen. Together they would share in that future. They were drawn together for a purpose.

He felt dizzy. He closed his eyes. His thoughts whirled. *This is it. Now I'm sure of it. The time has come to take control. Our destiny awaits. We've got to make it happen.* The breeze picked up, and he opened his eyes. Leaves and flower pedals swirled around the base of the statue. He gazed at the face of the glowing figure. "Virginia Dare," he said aloud. "You and I are about set sail for a new world."

The ringtone of his phone resounded, sending a charge through his already electrified body. He dug the iPhone out of his back pocket and glanced at the ID. Not recognizing the number, he slid his finger across the answer toggle and raised the phone to his ear. "Wes Wolf, here. Who am I talking to?"

A gravelly voice answered: "This is Alfred Bacon. I've decided I want in on this auction. Come back over to my place, and we'll talk."

A toothy grin widened Wolf's face. "I'll be there in ten minutes."

Chapter 16

Seeing the statue of Virginia Dare gave Wolf the confirmation he needed. The funny feeling in the pit of his stomach had faded. His headache was gone. Now he would focus one hundred percent on making this happen. *No reservations. No regrets. If I'm going to do this, I need to pull all stops. Take it to the limit.* His hands clenched the Cougar's steering wheel as he crossed the Washington Baum Bridge back to Roanoke Island. *Go big or go home.* The clichés became kindling to fuel the fire of determination burning within. *You can't get it all, unless you give it your all.* He expanded his chest with a deep breath and said, "Oh yeah. I'm going to swing for the fences."

He parked in the same space in front of the Cameron House Inn. Williard's Cascada and Alfred's Rolls Royce remained alongside the curb in front of the Cougar. He headed to the back of the Inn and saw Willard sitting on the steps of the annex building, smoking a cigarette. The punk jumped to his feet when he noticed Wolf approaching.

"Ahhh . . . It's my good friend, Willard Bacon." Wolf stopped directly in front of him and pointed to his cap. "One of these days I'm going to buy me one of those . . . to put on the scarecrow in my backyard."

Willard took a drag on his cigarette and blew a cloud of smoke into Wolf's face. "One of these days I'm going to pump bullets into your belly and watch you bleed like a slaughtered hog."

Wolf coughed, waved the smoke away and laughed. "That's if I ever give you your gun back."

"I've got plenty of guns."

"Yeah, but the one I took from you could put you behind bars for life."

The animosity on Willard's face faded into a malevolent stare. "More reason to turn you into maggot food."

"Are you sure you want to kill the goose before the golden egg arrives."

"What?"

Wolf pointed to the door. "Let's go see your uncle. He'll explain it to you."

Willard dropped his cigarette and stamped it out. "You're a damn goose alright, and I plan on ringing your neck." He led the way through the door and up the steps. Once inside the room, Willard leaned against the wall near the dresser.

Bacon sat in the same wicker chair against the opposite wall next to the window. He waved toward the chair by the desk. "Have a seat, Mr. Wolf. We need to talk again."

"I'm glad you're reconsidering. This kind of opportunity doesn't come along very often."

"That is true." Bacon folded his hands over his broad stomach. "It's a once in a lifetime chance to grab the brass ring."

Wolf nodded. "I'm here to give you that chance, but it'll cost you."

"I understand what you're saying. I've talked to my backers, and they're willing to fund my efforts. I believe with their support I can outbid Underdonk."

"Wait a minute." Wolf straightened and arched his back. "You're not even in the game yet. What I meant to say is that you need to pay the entry fee before I give you a ticket to the auction."

"Entry fee!" Bacon's thick eyebrows lowered. "What the hell are you talking about?"

"My dealer's fee. I want five thousand dollars in cash right now. That's the cover charge. Underdonk already paid."

Bacon spread his hands. "Where did you come up with this bullshit?"

Wolf stood. "Let me be clear." He thumbed over his shoulder at Willard. "Your flunky nephew over there has already threatened to kill me three times today. You need to tell him how foolish it would be to put my lights out before the diary arrives." He pointed at his own chest. "I'm the one who's delivering it. I'm putting my reputation and life on the line to conduct this crooked deal so that you or Underdonk can reap enough cabbage to buy the state of North Carolina. Tell him to lay off the threats. If he comes near me again, I swear I'll lay him out cold!"

"Relax. Sit down," Bacon ordered.

"I'm not going to sit down . . ." Wolf tapped his palm. ". . . until you put the dead presidents in my hand and call off your pit bull. Do it now, or I'm out the door!"

Bacon mumbled a few caustic curse words under his breath. "Willard, get me my checkbook out of the bottom drawer of the dresser."

Willard pushed off the wall and stood, stepped to the dresser and knelt. He opened the drawer and dug around until he found the checkbook. When he passed Wolf he sneered and nearly stepped on his foot. After handing the checkbook to his uncle, he sat down on the side of the bed, slumped his shoulders and stared out the window.

"Whoa!" Wolf said. "Tell the creep to lay off right now, or we're done here."

Bacon paused, pen and checkbook in hand, and gazed at Willard. "You heard the man. No more of this juvenile jabbering. Grow up."

Willard sat up straight and eyed his uncle like a teenage boy who just received his first Dear John letter.

"I'm not kidding around," Bacon said. "No more threats and stay away from Mr. Wolf." He shifted his focus back to Wolf. "Good enough?"

"It'll do." Wolf motioned toward Bacon. "I'd rather have cash than a check."

Bacon, writing out the check, glanced up. "You can go directly to the bank and cash this. I'll notify my financial institution about the transaction. There shouldn't be any problems. If so, call me, and I'll straighten it out." He finished writing the check and held it out to Wolf.

Wolf took several steps toward Bacon, swiped the check away, backed up and sat down. After inspecting the figure on the check, he said, "Okay, you're in. Now we need to go over a few details."

"Yes, like where and when."

"We could do it right here, if you don't mind. We're in the back of the inn in a separate building. You have your own private entrance. I don't think anybody will bother us or interfere with our proceedings."

Bacon raised and lowered his chin. "That's fine. What time?"

"The diary is arriving tomorrow afternoon. Virginia's father will let her know where and when. Let's meet here about noon. The diary will be delivered by boat, and I'm the only one authorized to pick it up. The public docks are only a couple blocks from here. It shouldn't take me more than ten minutes to retrieve the diary and get back here."

"You're sure the boat will dock over at the Shallowbag Bay Marina? Seems *too* public to me."

"I don't know for sure. It would be the easiest place to dock, but you may be right. That boat could pull up almost anywhere around the island. Wherever it docks, I'll go get it."

Bacon rubbed his hands together slowly and then clasped them in front of him. "What about the auction? Is it just Underdonk and me? Do we get a chance to inspect the diary?"

"It'll be just the two of you. Have you seen the certified reports on the diary pages Thomas Ellis had tested for proof of authentication?"

"Yes. I met with Ellis, and he showed me the reports and the diary. That's why I'm here. I trust its authenticity and know what it looks like. I want the chance to inspect it before I bid."

"That's not a problem." Wolf waved two fingers at Bacon. "A couple more things: we will not hand the diary over to the winning bidder until the funds have been transferred and are secured."

"I assumed that would be the procedure."

"Good." Wolf leaned forward on his knees. "Secondly, I'm assuming you know that the diary was stolen."

Bacon's eyes narrowed. "Ellis never told me how he acquired it."

"It was hidden in a house that once belonged to his ancestors. The owners didn't know it was there. Frank Fregiotto broke in one night and stole it. Now you know."

Bacon grunted. "So if I win the bid, I'll be marketing a stolen item."

"Correct."

"But the owners of the house don't know it was stolen?"

"Right, but they may become suspicious. A security camera caught Fregiotto carrying a box out of the house. Ellis convinced the owners it was on old book he had left behind. He worked out a deal with them to have the charges dropped."

"I see." Bacon rubbed his chin. "If the owners don't know where I acquired the diary, there shouldn't be a problem."

"Exactly. That's why you need to keep your mouth shut whether you win or lose. We all know this is a shady deal. No one is innocent here. If one of us goes down, we all go down."

The lines on Bacon's forehead deepened. "I'm not a stoolie. I live by a strict code. You make sure you keep *your* mouth shut."

Wolf waved dismissively at him. "Don't worry about me. I've got too much to lose." Wolf stood and stretched. "Any more questions? It's been a long day."

Bacon stood with surprising agility considering his girth. "One more thing. When do we get Willard's gun back?"

Wolf stifled a sardonic grin. "I wondered when you'd get around to that."

Willard arose from the bed and faced Wolf with questioning eyes.

"If you win the bid, I'll give the gun back after the funds are transferred. If you don't win the bid, I'm keeping the gun for insurance purposes."

Bacon glanced at Willard and then refocused on Wolf. "Fair enough. I plan on winning the bid."

Wolf pointed at Willard and grinned. "That would certainly help Gatsby Boy sleep easier at night."

Willard stepped forward to say something, but Bacon held up his hand. "Muzzle it."

"That reminds me," Wolf said. "I don't want Gatsby Boy up here during the auction. I don't trust him, and I can't stand him. He can wait outside and smoke cigarettes 'til he turns blue, but I don't want him in this room."

Bacon nodded. "That's fine." He turned to Willard. "You can hang out on the porch and keep watch. Make sure nobody snoops around."

"Don't sweat it," Willard said. "I've got it covered."

"Right," Wolf said. "With you on the job we'll all rest easier." He headed for the door and under his breath muttered, "What a jerk."

Once Wolf climbed into the Cougar, he checked his watch—5:30. On Friday the banks around town stayed open until six. He drove a couple blocks to the First National Bank on Sir Walter Raleigh Street. He turned into the drive-through and stopped in front of the customer access intercom. He snatched the container from the pneumatic tube base and undid the clasp to get to the pen. He quickly signed the check, told the cashier that he wanted cash, all in hundreds, and sent the container on its way. While he waited, he shifted in his seat and slipped his phone out of his back pocket to call Virginia. *Dammit! The battery's dead.* He didn't have a charger in the car. He wanted to tell her about the meeting with Bacon and get any updates from her father. He decided to head over to Angie's place in Nags Head to see her. After about five minutes the bank finally cashed the check, no questions asked. *That was easy enough.* He wedged his wallet into his front pocket and patted it. Wow. *All those C-notes make for a snug fit.*

From Manteo it took less than ten minutes to get to Angie's house just north of the golf course in Nags Head. He noticed an empty driveway as he pulled in and wondered why Angie's Honda Civic wasn't parked there. She usually quit work about five. *Maybe she stopped to pick up groceries on the way home.* A foreboding sensation threatened to invade his consciousness, but he shook it off.

He exited the car, hurried up the steps and rapped on the door. It swung open, and Virginia stood there in a loose-fitting green tunic and jeans. The shirt was unbuttoned halfway down creating a deep vee that stretched to her breastbone. Wolf drew in a deep breath and took in her beauty. He felt a fire rising inside and wanted to pull her down onto the living room floor and make love to her. He stepped inside and they embraced. He ran his hands up and down her back, feeling the curve of her body through the thin fabric. They kissed passionately. After what seemed like more than a minute, they separated, breathing rapidly.

"I'm so glad you're here," Virginia gasped. "I was about to call you."

"Did you hear from your father?"

"Yes. He wants me to send a picture of you and get a description of the clothes you'll be wearing tomorrow."

"That's a good idea," Wolf said. "He's a smart guy. He doesn't want to hand the diary over to an imposter."

"He thinks about all of those possibilities and always has a backup plan." She grabbed his hand, led him to the middle of the living room and positioned him under the brass-framed light mounted on the ceiling. "There. That's perfect." She backed away, snatched her phone from the coffee table and activated the camera app.

Wolf raised his hands. "Don't shoot!" He used his fingers to comb through his thick sandy hair, hoping to gather and smooth it to look presentable. "I don't want your father to think I'm some bum you ran into under a bridge."

She laughed and took the photo. "That's a silly thing to say."

"Tell him I'll be wearing a black Polo shirt with my agency logo in yellow and black dress pants."

"How many of those black shirts do you own?"

"A bunch." Wolf rubbed the logo on the left side of his chest. "I'll be getting another batch soon with a new logo."

She frowned and said, "Poor Mr. Bain. I can't help thinking it's my fault that he's gone, and your business has been shaken up."

"Don't worry about it. Bain is dead because of his own incompetence. Besides, he's not upset. When you're dead, you don't even know it."

She gave him a perturbed glare. "That's an odd way to look at it."

"It's the truth. Life is for the living." He pulled her to him and grasped her shoulders. "You and I are fully alive."

She smiled and took in a deep breath. "I feel like we're at the beginning of something amazing."

"Do you want to hear something amazing?"

"Sure."

"Earlier today I was walking through the woods, thinking about all this. I saw a glowing figure of a woman, nude and beautiful, staring off into the future."

Her eyes widened. "Who was it?"

"It was you."

She laughed. "I hate to break the news to you, but I've been here ever since you dropped me off."

He kissed her quickly on the forehead. "It was a statue of you—the Virginia Dare statue along one of the paths in the Elizabethan Gardens."

Wolf felt a shiver go through her body and her arms tighten around his waist. She said, "That's a sign!" She met his gaze. "But you don't believe in signs, do you?"

"I'm beginning to. When I saw the statue, something clicked inside. I knew we had been drawn together for a purpose. We're going to make this thing happen tomorrow, and our lives will never be the same."

She grasped the back of his head and kissed him. "Weston Wolf . . . I . . . I love you."

He clasped her face in his hands. "I love you, too, Virginia Dare. This is the beginning of a great adventure. You and I are going to take on a couple scoundrels and walk away with millions."

Her eyes lit with excitement. "If we succeed, you won't have to buy any more black Polo shirts."

Her words were like an unfamiliar song. "I guess that's true. Now that I think about it, my investigative career will be over." He wasn't sure if he liked the tune.

"How did your meeting with Albert Bacon go?"

"I had to break out the sledgehammer."

"That doesn't sound good."

"A guy like Bacon can't see the light unless you break down the wall of pride that's blocking his view. It took a couple of trips and some heavy hitting, but I knocked the wall down."

"He's willing to compete with Underdonk?"

Wolf nodded. "At first he told me to go to hell, and I left. Then he called and changed his mind. He managed to round up financial support from his so-called backers."

She turned her head and stared blankly beyond him. "He has connections with some dangerous people in Charlotte. If he wins the bid, they will expect a huge cut of the profits. Knowing Bacon, I can tell you he's not happy about this. He'd much rather steal the diary and take all the mash potatoes and gravy for himself."

He pressed the palm of his hand against her cheek and swiveled her head back toward him. "That's why you hired me: to keep him on a strict diet."

"Be careful, Wes. He doesn't play games." She planted the side of her face against his chest and wrapped her arms around him, squeezing him tightly. "We've just begun our journey. I don't want it to end before we barely get started."

He rubbed her back gently. "I can handle Bacon and his delinquent nephew. As far as our journey goes, we can only take it one minute at a time."

She raised her head, and their eyes met. "All we really have are these moments now."

"That's right. We'll make the most of this day and worry about tomorrow when it gets here. I want to spend tonight with you."

"Really?"

He smiled and kissed her softly on the lips. "I'm going to go home and take a shower. Then I'll come back and pick you up. We'll go out to dinner and then find a room somewhere and spend the night together."

"Oh, Wes, that would be wonderful! I'll take a hot bath and get all my things ready. Let's relish every minute we share this evening."

The sound of a car turning into the driveway interrupted them.

Wolf broke away from the embrace, stepped toward the door and opened it. "It's just Angie." He watched her get out of the car and walk toward the house. Her usual sassy smile had been replaced with tight lips and tense eyes.

He stepped onto the porch. "What's the matter, Angel? Is everything alright?"

She halted at the bottom of the steps and glared at him, her face drained of its color. "I've been trying to call you for the last hour."

"My phone died."

"You're not going to believe what happened."

Chapter 17

Wolf couldn't imagine what had happened, but he knew it wasn't good. Virginia stepped onto the porch beside him. Whatever it was, he knew he had to deal with it. *This better not wreck everything for tomorrow.* He steadied himself. "Okay, tell me what happened."

Angie, standing at the bottom of the few steps, gazed up at him with hollow eyes. "Laura Bain stopped in again this afternoon."

Wolf hung his head, sloped his shoulders and let out a disgusted exhale. He raised up and fixed his eyes on Angie. "Did you tell her to get lost?"

Angie nodded. "I told her everything you told me to tell her: That it was over and you didn't want to see her anymore; that you couldn't stand her and to stay away from you and the office."

Virginia put her hand on Wolf's shoulder, her eyes somewhat astonished. "That was quite harsh, don't you think?"

"It had to be done," Wolf said. "The woman sucks the blood out of you like a fat tick. Sometimes you just have to yank it out."

Angie blew out a soft whistle. "She got yanked out of your life alright."

"What did she do?" Wolf asked.

"She collapsed right there in the office and cried for fifteen minutes. It was horrible. Finally, I had to pull her to her feet and tell her to leave."

"Well . . ." Wolf took a breath and blew it out. "At least it's over now."

Angie shook her head. "It's not over."

Wolf stiffened, a feeling of dread filtering through him from his chest down into his legs. "What do you mean?"

"An hour later I got a call from the Outer Banks Hospital. She slit her wrists."

"No!" Wolf closed his eyes, and his head lurched back as if his neck muscles had gone slack. Opening his eyes, he saw the fading blue of the sky. "Is she . . . is she dead?"

"No. She's in intensive care."

Wolf straightened and clasped his hands on top of his head. "What is wrong with that woman?" Images of their brief affair played through his mind like a preview of some tawdry romance movie. He had responded to her advances purely out of lust, but she had fallen hard for him. But what could he do about it? He made the mistake and regretted it. Shame washed over him. "Why did they call us?"

"Because she wants to see you."

Wolf didn't know what to say. The contempt he'd felt toward Laura Bain had bled away from the gash that guilt had torn in his conscience.

"Now you know how I feel," Virginia said. "I blame myself for her husband's death. It's a terrible thing to feel responsible for what happens to people."

"Neither one of you are to blame," Angie said. "This is a rotten world, and people make bad decisions. Nobody is perfect. It is what it is."

Wolf gained some composure. "Why did she want to see me? I should be the last person on her list."

"She said she had something important to tell you."

Wolf's mind rambled through the possibilities. "What more could she tell me? I don't want to hear how much she loves me again."

Angie shrugged. "Who knows? The hospital attendant felt it was serious enough to make the phone call."

Wolf rubbed his knuckles against the growth of beard on his jaw. *What else could it be? Knowing Laura, I'm guessing she's throwing a Hail Mary. But then again, maybe not.* Wolf turned to Virginia. "I've got to go to the hospital and see her."

"Of course," she said. "I understand completely."

"I don't know how long this will take. We may have to postpone our date."

Virginia put her hands on his shoulders. "That's not a problem. If we can't go out for dinner tonight, we can celebrate tomorrow after the sale. Go see Mrs. Bain and do what you can to comfort her."

"I'm coming with you," Angie said. "I feel bad about what's happened. She seems like a lost soul. I want to tell her I'm sorry for the harsh words I said."

Wolf turned to Angie. "Didn't you just tell us that no one is to blame?"

"Yeah," Angie sighed. "I guess guilt is contagious."

The Outer Banks Hospital was only a few minutes away. As Wolf turned south onto Croatan Highway, Angie said, "Poor Laura, she's gone completely off the rails."

"She must feel totally lost. George couldn't fill that emptiness in her life. After Fregiotto killed him, she hoped that I would be the one to make her complete. Making women feel whole isn't one of my strong points."

"I don't count on a man to make me feel good about myself. I take responsibility for who I am."

"Good for you."

"What if it wasn't Fregiotto? What if *she* killed her husband to marry you? Then she tried to shift the blame to you when you rejected her."

"You're thinking like a good detective, but like I told you before, Laura doesn't have the guts to kill anyone."

"How can you say that? She just tried to kill herself. Taking someone's life can weigh heavy on you. As far as we know, she doesn't have an alibi. Remember, I saw her entering her house the night I went to tell her about George's death."

"So you think she wants to confess to murder?"

"It's a possibility. Until proven otherwise, I won't discount it." Angie lifted a large canvas purse from her lap and set it on the floor of the car. "Make sure you lock your doors. I don't want to take my purse in with me."

Wolf turned into the hospital parking lot. "When did you get that behemoth?"

"Yesterday. My conceal and carry license just arrived in the mail today."

"Whoa!" Wolf pulled into an empty space near the front of the lot and cut the engine. He faced Angie. "You mean to tell me you're carrying a .357 Magnum revolver in that purse?"

"That's why I needed a bigger purse. You better leave your gun here. They've got signage at the entrance and a metal detector."

He lifted his shirt, removed his Sig Sauer from the holster and slid it under his car seat. "Now I feel naked."

Angie shook her head. "Now that's a disturbing image."

Wolf hated hospitals: the smell of disinfectant, the echoing of footsteps down the hallways, the murmuring of the staff, the beeps and buzzes of medical machinery, and the sounds of the sick and suffering coming from patient rooms. The atmosphere reminded him of his own mortality. When Death came knocking on his door, he hoped for a swift and unexpected end. To Wolf, a lingering death in a hospital or nursing home would be unbearable. He'd rather take a bullet to the brain or drive off a cliff.

He had avoided hospitals most of his life. When he was ten, he took a tumble on his skateboard and cut his chin wide open. It took fifteen stiches and left a nasty scar that was still visible. That was the last time he was in an emergency room.

When close friends or family were hospitalized, he'd make the obligated visit, but otherwise he stayed away.

He and Angie arrived at the Intensive Care Unit, and a receptionist instructed them to have a seat in the waiting room where a physician would soon give them an update. Four other people sat spaced out around the room. They read magazines or watched the NBC Nightly News broadcast from a flat screen TV mounted on a nearby wall. Lester Holt warned residents of the Gulf Coast to prepare for a hurricane that would soon arrive with sustained winds of more than 100 mph. Wolf hoped it wouldn't turn east and smack the Outer Banks with flooding rains. They had more than their share of hurricanes and tropical storms, usually two or three a year.

"What's going on tomorrow?" Angie said. "Miss Dare mentioned some kind of sale."

Wolf realized he had been fairly close-lipped concerning his dealings with the Dare Diary transaction. He trusted Angie. How much should he tell her? "Virginia Dare hired me to conduct an auction tomorrow."

"Maybe I should add that to our new sign: Wolf and Stallone Detective Agency and Auctioneering Service."

"Let's wait and see how it goes."

Her eyes narrowed. "Sounds like there may be some risk to this so-called sale."

He bobbed his head. "There's definitely some risk."

"Is Underdonk invited?"

Wolf nodded.

"When he pulled that pistol on you, I had to step in and take care of things."

Wolf raised a finger. "And I truly appreciate that."

"Then you warned me to keep my eye out for Gatsby Boy and his silver Cascada. I know you had some kind of meeting with his boss."

"That would be Alfred Bacon. He'll be at the auction too."

"Then there's Virginia Dare, the mysterious charlatan from Charlotte. I wouldn't trust her to hold my beer while I tied my shoe."

"She's been somewhat deceitful, but I kinda like her."

"You more than like her. I've never seen you this far gone over a woman. Do you know what the words fatal attraction mean?"

Wolf chuckled. "Don't get carried away. She's a client. She hired me to pick up the heirloom, deliver it to the sale and manage the auction."

Angie rubbed her chin. "And this heirloom would be . . . the Dare Diary?"

Wolf sat quietly for several seconds. "That is correct. You are growing in your perceptive keenness. Those classes must be paying off."

"Uh huh." Angie crossed her arms. "When I sum all this up, these questionable characters plus a priceless diary, the bottom line alarms me. This meeting may be hazardous to your health."

Wolf faced her, sensing a growing seriousness in her tone. "You're right. This could be hazardous to my health and my reputation."

She placed her hands on top of her legs and leaned toward him. "Then why are you doing it?"

"With great risks come big paydays. Angel, if I can pull this off, I may never have to work again."

"I see." She stared blankly at the tiled floor. "If that's what you want, then I better hold off on ordering those signs."

Wolf sat quietly for a minute. "I don't know if that's what I want."

The double ICU doors powered open, and a man wearing black-framed glasses and a white lab coat approached them. A stethoscope hung around his neck. He looked to be about forty with short, black hair combed straight back.

He stopped a few feet away. "Mr. Wolf?"

"Yeah, I'm Wolf. This is Angie Stallone, my assistant."

"I'm Dr. Frazier. Thanks for coming. Mrs. Bain is resting peacefully at the moment. We had to give her a sedative."

"Is she going to be alright?" Angie asked.

"Physically, she'll make a full recovery. She lost a lot of blood, but we patched her up and gave her a little more than two quarts. The problem is her mental instability. That's why we called you. She seemed desperate to talk to you."

"When can I see her?" Wolf asked.

"We'd like to let her rest for an hour first. It was a strong sedative. Is that a problem?"

Wolf closed his eyes and shook his head. "I guess not. I mean, I had plans, but they can wait."

"Great. We want to do our best for her both physically and mentally. Do you know what she wants to talk to you about?"

"I have no idea."

The doctor eyed him as if he were assessing a peculiar mole. "Well . . . if you can think of anything that may help us deal with the anguish she's experiencing, please let us know."

"Sure thing, Doc."

He pivoted, strode to the wall near the double doors, pressed a big square button, and once the doors swung open, entered the ICU area.

"Can you believe it?" Wolf complained. "We've got to sit here another hour."

Angie sat back in the chair. "It might be the last hour we spend together."

"Listen, Angel, tomorrow is not guaranteed for me or you or anyone else. Who knows what will happen tomorrow?"

"You're right. I'm not counting on you for tomorrow. I'm just disappointed, that's all. If you hit it big and start a new life, I'll figure things out."

"I'm sure you will." Wolf sat back and crossed his ankles.

"Where is this sale going to take place?"

"At the Cameron House Inn about noon. There's an annex building behind the inn with an upstairs suite. Bacon and his nephew Willard are staying there. It should provide the privacy we need to conduct the auction."

"Do you have the Dare Diary?"

Wolf glanced at her and smiled. "No. Why are you so interested?"

"I might have to step in and rescue you again."

Wolf chuckled. "I thought you had a lunch date with young Deputy Thomas."

"I plan on making it a business lunch, just in case you need my help."

Wolf grinned and nodded. "Angel, you are a determined young lady, but I should be fine."

"If I'm your guardian angel, then I want to keep tabs on you."

"If I need you, I'll text or call."

"So where's the diary?"

"It will be delivered sometime tomorrow afternoon. Virginia will let me know where and when. Don't worry. I've got everything under control."

"Yeah, right. Whatever you say, Mr. Boss Man." Angie clasped her hands and rested them on her lap. She seemed to drift into her own thoughts, staring blankly at a medical poster on the opposite wall.

Wolf had to grapple with his own thoughts, too. He felt confident about tomorrow's proceedings, but nothing was guaranteed. Who knew what these shifty oddballs might do? He worried most about Alfred Bacon and young Willard.

With ties to the underworld, they felt extra pressure to pull off the winning bid and leave with the diary. That kind of pressure can force people to make desperate moves. *I need to be ready for anything. Keeping Willard outside will help me manage the situation. Should I start the bidding at twenty million? I hate to let it go for less than thirty. Let me see, if it goes for twenty, I'll make fifteen percent or three million dollars. If it goes for thirty, I'll make four and a half million.* Wolf rubbed his hands together. *That would be one helluva payday. I think I will require the opening bid to be no less than thirty million and see what they say. If they balk at my move, I'll keep pressing until they threaten to leave. It'll be like a game of chess. I need to play smart and not make any stupid moves. No, maybe I'll stick with twenty. Don't get greedy and blow this thing.*

He glanced at Angie. She still sat there staring at the wall. It was Friday night after a long week of work, and here she was, sitting next to him in a hospital waiting room. He had hired her three years ago right out of community college with her associate's degree in secretary science. He knew from the start that she was a great kid, dedicated and ambitious. Within six months of starting the job, she had begun taking law enforcement classes. Although she was only twenty-three years old, she seemed wise beyond her years. They had developed the kind of friendship that usually lasts a lifetime. Wolf wondered how much a successful sale would change things. He enjoyed his occupation—the independence, the cases, the importance of good instincts and decisions. He felt comfortable in his gumshoes. The money wasn't great, but tomorrow could change all that.

He glanced at Angie again. "You're awful quiet."

"Just thinking."

"About what?"

"What I'm going to do if you decide to quit the business. I'm thinking either the police academy or the military."

Wolf cleared his throat. "If I do retire young and fly off to Jamaica or Bermuda with Miss Dare, would you miss me?"

"Not a bit."

"Geesh! You didn't think twice about that answer."

Angie sniffed and rubbed her nose. "Don't have too. I can make it on my own." Her voice quavered slightly, and her eyes watered.

Wolf reached and grasped her hand. "I'd certainly miss you, young lady. I consider you one of my best friends."

She shook his hand away, crossed her legs and leaned away from him. "Quit it. You're just making things worse."

Wolf withdrew his arm. "Sorry. I'm not the most sensitive guy when it comes to women's feelings."

"Your lack of insight concerning women never ceases to amaze me."

"Well, don't start filling out applications yet. I don't know what I'm going to do if I hit the jackpot tomorrow."

"I just hope you don't end up in jail," she said, her tone becoming hard.

Wolf swallowed. "I'm with you there. Prison orange isn't my favorite color."

She glanced at him and shook her head. "Yeah, when life hands you an orange, be careful who's standing behind you in the shower."

Funny but true. Wolf gazed at the ceiling and frowned. *How did she know this deal was dirty? It wasn't filthy dirty, just dirty. I've gone over this again and again in my mind. It's worth the risk.* He took a quick look at Angie and then focused on the floor. *She's young and inexperienced. Give her some years in this business and she'll find out. When you're constantly dealing with corruption, it's hard not to get your hands dirty.* He glanced at her again. She had shifted in her seat, watching an episode of *Jeopardy* on the big screen TV. *No, I'm wrong. She'd never do what I'm going to do tomorrow, not Angel. She'd play by the book.*

After *Jeopardy*, they watched *Wheel of Fortune*. One of the answers to the hidden phrases was CRIME DOESN'T

PAY. Wolf had to laugh. This afternoon, all the signs had pointed to yes. Tonight, they pointed to no. *The hell with signs.* He decided to take it one step at a time and go with what seemed right in the moment. He checked his watch—almost eight o'clock. They'd been sitting there for an hour and a half. Angie elbowed him, and he glanced up. Dr. Frazier walked through the opening ICU doors and headed in their direction.

"Thank you so much for being patient," Dr. Frazier said. "She's awake and fairly clear-minded now, if you would like to see her."

Wolf stood. "That's why we're here."

Wolf and Angie followed him through the double doors past a nurse's station and a series of cubicles. Medical machines hummed and beeped. Red lights flashed from within the darkened patient chambers. Wolf saw silhouetted figures through the glass standing next to the beds. He assumed they were family members keeping watch over their loved ones or perhaps medical staff doing their best to preserve life.

The doctor stopped in front of cubicle 6, the large red number marking the glass door. "She needs her rest, so let's try to keep the visit to twenty minutes or so. If you encounter any problems, please let one of the attendants know. She's in a very unstable state, and we want to keep her as positive as possible."

"Sure thing, Doc," Wolf said. "We'll do our best to keep her spirits up."

With a stolid demeanor, Dr. Frazier opened the door. "Again, thanks for coming."

They entered the cubicle. Laura Bain lay on a raised bed, the sheet pulled up to her neck. A fluorescent light above the bed provided the only illumination in the room except for the medical monitors with their red and yellow flashing lights. Her hair was matted and stringy. She appeared to have aged ten years, shadows ringing her puffy eyes. Her lips trembled.

Wolf walked to the side of her bed, and Angie circled to the other side. She gazed up at him, slowly drew the sheet down and reached toward him. "Oh, Wes, I feel so ashamed."

He took her hand and noticed the bandages around her wrist. "I'm sorry, Laura. I didn't mean for this to happen."

She shook her head and blinked. A tear trickled down her cheek. "It's not your fault. There's something wrong with me."

"You've been through a lot over these last few days," he said.

"I go through these crazy moods. One minute I feel like I'm going to be okay, but the next it feels like the devil is pulling me down into a deep hole."

He squeezed her hand. "I didn't know how bad you were feeling, or I wouldn't have cut you off like I did."

"I don't blame you." She shifted her gaze to door. "I acted horribly. I don't know what got into me. My life has been so empty for years."

Angie laid her hand gently on Laura's shoulder. "George's death must have been difficult for you."

She swallowed. "Yes. Despite all our fights and failures, it hit me hard. I hated him, and I loved him."

Wolf said, "He wasn't the ideal husband."

"I know he ran around on me, but I wasn't a saint myself. I had affairs just to get even with him." She shifted her focus to Wolf. "You were the only one who made me feel different. I thought there was a chance with you."

"Laura, I'm no better than George. I'm sorry I took advantage of you just for the pleasure of a night between the sheets."

"Come on now, Wes. I led you on. I took a chance with you. I couldn't accept that it wasn't to be. Now I know."

"But I was mean to you, and I feel bad about it."

She took a deep breath and exhaled audibly. "I guess it's like the Bible says: we're all sinners."

Wolf smiled. "Ain't that the truth."

"I need to apologize to you for accusing you of my husband's murder. I was in one of those moods. When I realized you didn't feel the way I felt, I saw red. I wanted to hurt you, and that's the only way I knew how. Can you forgive me?"

"Of course. Let's forgive and forget. We'll toss those sins into the Atlantic Ocean and send them out with the tide."

She smiled weakly. "This afternoon I was ready to die, but now I'm feeling better. I go up and down like a yo-yo."

Angie leaned forward, "Laura, there's medication that can help you manage those feelings."

She turned toward Angie. "That's what the doctor said. If I get out of this hole, I'm going to get on the right medicine and get back on the road to recovery."

"We're here to be your friend and give you support," Angie said.

Laura bobbed her head slowly. "Thanks. I need friends." She gazed up at Wolf. "Don't worry. I'm not going to expect any more from you than friendship."

"We'll keep it at that level. I'm a better friend than a lover."

Laura laughed. "I learned that the hard way."

"Laura, I wanted to apologize to you," Angie said. "I treated you terribly this afternoon. I spoke harshly and made you leave the office when I should have had compassion."

"No." She shook her head. "You were dealing with a mad woman. I don't blame you. There's nothing you could have said to make any difference."

"It wasn't Angie's fault," Wolf said. "I told her to keep you away from me. She was following orders. Now I know better."

Laura squeezed his hand. "Hopefully, we all know better."

Wolf said, "I'm glad we had this chance to talk."

"Making amends always makes things better," Angie said.

Laura reached and took Angie's hand. "There's healing in forgiveness. Thank you both for coming. You've propped me up and made me smile."

Angie rubbed the top of Laura's hand. "Was there something else you wanted to tell us."

Laura nodded and pulled her hands away from both of them. "The night my husband was murdered, I did something."

Wolf leaned closer. "What do you mean, Laura? What did you do?"

"Like I said, I loved him and hated him. When he went out that night, I became jealous. I figured he was having another affair."

Wolf shook his head. "George was on an assignment. He was tailing the guy that shot him."

Laura's lips tightened into a line across her face. The fluorescent light cast a ghostly pale on her forehead and cheeks.

Angie leaned a few inches closer. "On the night your husband was murdered, I stopped by your house to break the news to you. When I parked my car, I noticed you had just returned home. You were on your porch, unlocking the door. Where did you go that night?"

Her eyes seemed to see through the wall to another place and time. "I was suspicious of him and wanted to catch him in the act. After he went out the door, I followed him."

Chapter 18

The morning sun broke over the edge of the ocean and beamed into Wolf's bedroom window. He turned over and clasped a pillow against his head to shield his eyes from the rays. *Too early to get up. I'm not ready to think about today's exploits.* He tried to go back to sleep, but the possibilities kept revolving through his mind. He needed to be ready for anything that could go wrong. Counting on things running smoothly would be foolish. He had promised himself to make the best decisions moment by moment. Going over the various outcomes provided ammunition for those split-second decisions. He needed to be as sharp as a new razorblade, but a poor night's sleep threatened to dull his mental acuity. If only he could blank his mind and catch some more shuteye. He closed his eyes and tried to drift off to Slumberland, but the faces of Hugh Underdonk, Alfred Bacon, Willard Bacon and Virginia Dare kept appearing out of the darkness.

Last night's visit with Laura Bain had thrown him out of rhythm too. Her suffering disheartened him and drained away any enthusiasm he had stored up for today's proceedings. He recognized he was partially to blame for her breakdown. Fortunately, they had reconciled and came to a clear understanding of the nature of their relationship. They would be friends and nothing more. He hoped she would embrace those terms and not go down that dark path again. By the time he returned home from the hospital, he knew spending the night with Virginia was no longer a promising prospect. He called her and apologized for his change of mood. She said she understood. Too many unanswered questions nagged him.

One of those questions was what would happen to his relationship with Angie Stallone. She was probably the most solid, dependable person in his life. He treasured their friendship and knew she valued it as much as he. How does that kind of relationship weigh on the scale of life when balanced against incredible wealth? She told him she would go in a new direction if he struck it rich. Losing someone that close could be demoralizing. If it was up to her, they would become partners and build the business together. That would be interesting and . . . challenging. *Do I really want to get rich and travel the world with a beautiful lady? That seems like a rhetorical question. Of course, I do . . . maybe.*

He thought about that lady. Should falling in love with someone completely change his direction in life? Was he truly in love with Virginia Dare? He'd never felt this way before about another woman. She was beautiful, determined, daring and smart. But she was also deceptive, cunning and vicious toward her enemies. Wolf wondered if he was attracted to her positive attributes as well as the negative ones. *Did I fall in love with her because she is a lot like . . . me?* That was an odd conclusion. Maybe it was true. If so, was that a good basis for a long-term relationship? Only time could answer those questions. He had known so many couples who believed their romance would last a lifetime but floundered after a few years on the seas of adversity. *But didn't love demand that we climb into the boat and set sail. If we're not willing to unhitch from the dock of familiar routine and head out to sea, how will we ever know?*

He tossed and turned for the next two hours, drifting in and out of sleep. At 8:30 he arose and staggered to the kitchen to put on the coffee and fix a bowl of cornflakes with a sliced banana. After eating breakfast, he poured another cup of coffee and headed to his office. Glancing at his desk, he spotted the book he had purchased at the bookstore in Manteo—*The Lost Colony and their Journey to Croatoan*. He settled into his swivel chair, picked up the book and began to read where he had left off.

He read for an hour and a half, amazed at the courage of the colonists. They did not expect their lives to unravel so perilously in the New World. After only a few weeks on Roanoke Island they realized they were in big trouble. Sending Eleanor's father, John White, back to England for supplies offered their best hope of survival. Then they faced hunger, constant threat of attack, drought, a bitter winter and disease. When White didn't return within a year, they had to make a move. Wherever they went, they knew death awaited at every turn. But they packed up and headed for Croatan Island where the natives were more friendly. Only a few survived and lived out their lives in the wilderness of this new land.

Wolf tossed the book onto the desk, leaned back in his chair and clasped his hands behind his head. *Were they brave or stupid? Or both? They had high hopes of adventure and dreams of prosperity. If they didn't climb into the boat and set sail, how would they ever know? They found out the hard way. The question is: Knowing what awaited them in the New World, how many would choose differently? Probably most if not all of them.* Wolf marveled at the irony of his situation. Today's venture demanded great risk based on a diary written by one of those colonists who went all in on the gamble. *Will I end up like Eleanor Dare? He shrugged. At least she survived.* He glanced at his watch—11:05. He needed to get ready and head over to Angie's to pick up Virginia.

As he drove along Barracuda Road he watched a white Ford F150 pickup turn into Angie's driveway just ahead of him. He pulled up along the left side of the vehicle and parked. Deputy Joel Thomas swung open the truck door and stepped out. His blue denim shirt hung loosely over tight-fitting jeans. He wasn't a big man, maybe six feet tall and 170 pounds. Wolf wasn't used to seeing him without his black law enforcement ball cap. His light brown hair was buzzed on the sides but longer and combed back on top.

Wolf got out of the Cougar, smiled and gave him pseudo salute.

"Hey, Wes, I didn't expect to see you today," Deputy Thomas said. "Did you need to talk to Angie about something?"

"No. My girlfriend has been staying here a few days. I came to pick her up."

"Angie mentioned she had a guest. She didn't say much about her, though. Is it the same girl I met at your office a couple nights ago and at the Blue Moon yesterday? I think you said her name was Emma Ritz."

"That's right, Joel." Wolf raised a finger. "A good memory is an excellent asset for an investigator. You ought to consider becoming a detective."

Deputy Thomas grinned. "I plan on it. Every day is a step in that direction."

Wolf noticed a slight bulge under Joel's shirt. "Are you carrying on your day off?"

Deputy Thomas patted his side. "Glock 19. Always be ready to protect and serve."

The kid sounds like me back in the day. Wolf patted his black Polo shirt where the Sig Sauer was strapped to his side. "Better to be prepared than surprised."

"I'll second that. Hey, we're headed over to the Shaddai Restaurant in Manteo for lunch. They've got great Peruvian food. You and your girlfriend are welcome to join us."

"Thanks for the invite, but we've got our own plans."

Deputy Thomas shrugged. "Maybe next time."

"Maybe. How's Sheriff Walton doing? Making any progress on the murder investigations?"

Deputy Thomas grimaced. "Not really. He still thinks you killed one or the other. He just can't prove it."

"What do you think?"

He raised an eyebrow. "I think you know a lot more than he does."

"You are a sharp-minded lawman. I might have to recommend you for a promotion. That's if good ol' Sheriff Walton will pay attention to someone with common sense." Wolf skirted around the car and slapped Deputy Thomas on the back. "Let's go see what our girls are up to."

They climbed the steps and crossed the porch. Wolf rapped on the door.

A few seconds later the door opened, and Angie appeared wearing a burnt orange summer dress with a strap on one shoulder and a sleeve on the other. It was rather short and unevenly cut but cute. "Surprise, surprise, it's Mr. Boss Man and Deputy Joel," she said.

"Hey, Angie, I like the dress," Deputy Thomas said.

"Thanks, Joel."

"Yes." Wolf took a step back. "It looks quite . . . asymmetrical."

She shook her head. "Like your face." She stepped aside. "Come on in, boys."

"Where's Emma?" Wolf asked.

"Who?" Angie gave him a questioning stare. "Oh . . . yeah . . . Emma. She's in the bathroom getting spruced up for you."

"Did you forget her name?" Deputy Thomas asked.

Angie laughed. "No. I call her by another name." She waved her hand. "One that I won't repeat."

Deputy Thomas raised his eyebrows and glanced at Wolf.

"You know how women can be in close quarters," Wolf jeered, "like two cats in burlap sack."

Angie slugged him in the stomach, and he let an "Oooooofffff." She said, "That's the comment I get when I do you a big favor?"

"My apologies," he groaned, rubbing his midsection. "I do owe you big for helping us out."

"Yeah, you do, but I'm not counting on the payoff I deserve. Do you want to know what I call her? The Gold Dust Woman, and you're the hired hand to dig up the lode. I just hope you're not digging your own grave."

Wolf swallowed. "Don't get mad at me, Angel. She'll be gone before you get back. Who knows where I'll end up? Hopefully, in a better place."

"Well . . . heaven's a better place, but there's no hurry to get there." She raised her chin, and stiffened her lower lip. "You make sure you text me or call me if you need me."

"I will."

She picked up her beige canvas purse from the yellow rocking chair, hoisted the strap over her shoulder, and linked her arm through the crook of Deputy Thomas's elbow. "Let's go, Joel. I want to stop by the hardware store before we go out to eat." She motioned across the living room. "I need to pick up some disinfectant and bug spray to give this place a good going-over when I get back."

Geesh, Virginia must have really rattled her cage. "Have a nice day," Wolf said gingerly.

As they headed for the door, Deputy Thomas gave Wolf a bewildered look over his shoulder. "We'll see you later, Wes. You take care now."

"Sure thing, Joel. I plan on it." Once they were out the door he said, "As careful as a snake handler milking a rattler."

Wolf plopped down on the green-plaid couch and picked up a detective magazine from the coffee table. The main article displayed in large red letters on the cover read: **AVOIDING AN AMBUSH** – page 53. *That's a must read.* Wolf flipped to the page. He scanned down through the introduction to the first tip highlighted with bold letters. *Let's see, helpful hint number 1 –* **PUT YOUR CELL PHONE AWAY**. *That makes sense. Playing Candy Crush may crush your hopes of survival. Number 2 –* **NOTICE WHEN SOMETHING IS OUT OF PLACE**. *Okay, if I see a guy coming at me with a butcher knife,*

I'll sit up and pay attention. Number 3 – APPROACH ALL SITUATIONS WITH STEALTH. That's not a problem. I'm a stealthy guy. Number 4 – COMPLACENCY KILLS. Hmmmm . . . thinking that'll never happen to me could be lethal. Number 5 – DON'T BE MISDIRECTED. Now that's a good one. The bullet that tears through your heart may come from an unexpected direction.

"What are you reading?" Virginia Dare stepped beside him.

He glanced up. Willowy, cool and incredibly sexy, she wore a white blouse with a prim collar and pink cutoff shorts with red hearts embroidered on the pockets. Her short and sassy black hair, full red lips and exquisite body fanned the flame of desire within him. He wanted to reach out and run his hand up and down those long, milky legs. *Whoa, boy. Don't get carried away.* He flipped the magazine onto the coffee table and stood. "Just brushing up on some safety tips for today's meeting."

"Any good ones I should know about?"

He pulled her to him and kissed her eagerly and roughly. When they parted, he said, "How about – Approach all situations with stealth."

She smiled slyly. "Sounds like wise advice."

Wolf checked his watch – 11:45. "I wish we had time to make up for last night."

"That would be nice, but we'll have plenty of time after the sale. We can more than make up for it tonight."

Wolf ran his hands down her back and across her hips. "Business before pleasure."

"Yes." She reached and patted his cheek with solid taps. "Let's take care of business first. When our bank accounts are full, then we'll get our fill of each other."

Wolf released his embrace and waved toward the door. "It's almost high noon, and the customers are waiting."

"My bags are packed and in the bedroom. I'd rather load up now and not come back here."

"Too bad you and Angie didn't get along. She's a great gal."

Virginia shrugged and gave an indulgent smile. "She didn't like me from the beginning. Perhaps she feels that I'm a threat."

"Don't feel bad. She never has approved of my taste in women." Wolf turned, hurried into the bedroom, lifted a green tote bag by its long strap and slipped it over his shoulder. Then he picked up her two tan suitcases and carried them into the living room. "I think I've got everything."

"Onward to our New World." She picked up her large leather shoulder bag and headed for the door.

Wolf loaded the baggage into the trunk while Virginia climbed onto the passenger seat. He got into the car, backed it out of the driveway and onto the street. *Here we go, setting sail for Roanoke Island.*

Cruising along Croatan Highway, Wolf asked, "Have you heard from your father?"

"Not yet, but I'm sure he's on his way. He's driving across the state by himself to Edenton. That's where the first Dare Stone was found. He rented a boat there near the waterfront park. He insisted on piloting the boat alone across Albemarle Sound to Roanoke Island. I wish he weren't so obsessive about history and how he wants things done."

"He could have easily driven across the Manns Harbor Bridge."

She gave a short laugh. "No kidding. He doesn't always do things the easy way. He has odd ideas about how to honor the past. His ancestors arrived by boat and so will he."

"That's fascinating when you think about it," Wolf said. "He's returning the diary to the place where Eleanor Dare began writing it. I call that completing the circle of history."

"Now you're starting to sound like him."

"Maybe that's why you're attracted to me. I remind you of your father."

She reached and squeezed his quad. "I have my own reasons for being attracted to you."

"It's funny, isn't it?" Wolf rubbed the top of her hand. "Being attracted to someone doesn't follow any rhyme or reason. It just hits you like a sucker punch and down you go."

"For better or worse."

"I'm hoping for the better."

She removed her hand from his leg and said, "How did your visit with Mrs. Bain go last night?"

"Better than I expected. She seemed mentally stable. Of course, she was on sedatives. Hopefully, the doctor will prescribe a good medication to help her manage her mood swings. She apologized for accusing me of murdering her husband. She's knows I didn't do it."

"Did you love her?"

"No. We had one night together. Does that bother you?"

"A little. Was it a memorable night?"

"Yes, but once it was over, I knew I was there for all the wrong reasons."

"What about the night we spent together? How did you feel afterwards?"

"Like I wanted to see you again as soon as possible."

She put her hand back on his quad and squeezed gently. "Those are the words a lady likes to hear."

As they crossed the Washington Baum Bridge, Wolf said, "When I leave to get the diary, will you feel safe staying with Underdonk and Bacon?"

"As long as Willard keeps his distance."

"I'll remind Bacon to make Willard stay outside."

"He fears Alfred. Hopefully, he'll obey him."

"Both Bacon and Underdonk are smart enough to know that their opportunity to bid on the diary will depend on their good behavior. If they make any shifty moves, they'll risk that opportunity."

"Don't worry about me." She lifted her shoulder bag from her lap. "I've got a handgun in here. I've never fired it, but shooting a gun isn't brain surgery. Point and pull the trigger."

"Do you know what a safety is?"

"Of course." She lowered the bag and pulled out the .38 special. "It's this little lever on top of the handle, right?"

Wolf glanced over to see where she was pointing. "That's right. When I leave, reach into your purse and kick the safety off just in case something happens."

"Believe me, I'll defend myself if they try something."

"Remember, I saw you beat the hell out of Underdonk with his own cane. I know you've got the grit to kill someone if your life is threatened."

She threw her head back and laughed. "That was one of the highlights of my week. I'll never forget how shocked he looked when I grabbed his cane and thumped him. He cried like a little girl."

"You did seem to relish the moment."

She took a deep breath and blew it out. "Every whack of that cane was for Robert. If you and the sheriff hadn't stopped me, I would have beat him into unconsciousness."

Wolf wagged his head and smiled. "I don't think I'll be too worried about leaving you alone with those two scamps."

He turned right at the light onto Budleigh Street. "The Cameron House Inn is a couple blocks ahead. It's about showtime."

She fidgeted with the strap of her shoulder bag. "I'm getting nervous."

"There's nothing wrong with being nervous. Take a deep breath and try to relax."

She inhaled and exhaled slowly, wrung her hands and shook them out. "Oh boy. Here we go."

"Our ship is approaching the shore. Trust me, we've got this." Wolf pulled into an open parking space behind

Underdonk's deep-violet Jaguar and cut the engine. Ahead he could see Alfred's gray Rolls Royce and Willard's silver Cascada.

"Yeah, what could go wrong?" Virginia opened the door and stepped out of the car.

Wolf exited the Cougar, closed the car door and hurried around the back bumper to meet her on the sidewalk. They angled across the lawn toward the annex building in the rear. Walking past a huge pink-flowering azalea bush, they turned toward the breezeway. Virginia abruptly stopped and stiffened like a scared cat.

Wolf froze, eyes fixed on Willard Bacon. He sat on the breezeway steps loading a revolver.

Chapter 19

"The natives are restless," Virginia said.

Wolf took her hand. "He looks bored to me. Come on." They walked toward the breezeway. "I'll make his day."

They stopped in front of Willard, and he gazed up at them. "Whadayaknow?" he said. "It's the goose that's gonna lay the golden egg." He spun the cylinder of the revolver and then reached behind him and slid the gun into the back of his pants.

"You better be careful," Wolf said. "You might shoot another hole in your ass."

Willard drew a cigarette out of his front pocket and stuck it in the side of his mouth. "Naaa. I'll bet your life I don't. But later today I do plan on going goose hunting."

Wolf laughed. "Threats, bets and cigarettes. That's what little boys are made of."

Willard's jaw tensed and his lips tightened. The cigarette slipped out of his mouth and onto the ground. Wolf moved forward and stepped on it just as Willard leaned to get it. Willard's eyes caught fire, and he reached behind him for the gun.

Wolf raised his finger. "No, no, no, no, no. Hunting season hasn't started yet."

Willard eased the gun out and aimed it at Wolf's chest. "You're a dead goose walking."

Wolf grinned. "In that case, I'll walk on up the steps to meet with your uncle. We'll talk about your bad behavior and that murder weapon I took from you. Good luck with that goose hunt, Gatsby Boy. You'll need it."

Wolf led the way past Willard and across the breezeway to the entrance. He opened the door, and Virginia gave him a perturbed look as she entered. They ascended the stairs, and she whispered, "Try not to be so ingratiating next time."

Wolf chuckled. "I wasn't born to be nice. I came out kicking and screaming."

At the top of the stairway, they turned the corner past the bathroom and nook that housed the dresser. Wolf stepped to the side and let Virginia enter the large bedroom first. Underdonk, wearing his usual Brooks Brothers suit, sat in the wicker chair by the window, holding a whiskey tumbler glass half filled with ice and alcohol. Propped up on the bed with pillows, Bacon lounged with his legs stretched out on the rumpled cover. He wore a gray Nike sweat outfit and tan leather slippers.

"Good afternoon," Bacon grumbled. "The drinks are on the dresser around the corner. Help yourselves."

"Do you have any red wine?" Wolf asked.

"Wine, rum, whiskey, bourbon. Whatever you want."

Virginia murmured, "I'll pour us a couple glasses of wine." She peeled away and turned the corner toward the dresser.

Wolf spread his hands. "Nice day for an auction— sunny skies and jolly guys."

Underdonk swirled the ice in his glass. "I'll be jollier when the diary gets here."

Wolf eyed Underdonk and rubbed his chin. "How many of those purple suits do you own?"

"I have a whole closetful," he wheezed.

Wolf grinned. "Purple *is* a royal color."

"And one day I'll be king."

"More like queen," Bacon chortled.

Underdonk sneered, "And there you are, Mr. Bacon, all dressed up for the occasion wearing a sweat suit and slippers. You look like a retired gym teacher."

Bacon clasped his hands over his stomach. "I like to be comfortable when I'm competing. Who knows how long we'll be waiting for the diary to get here? I choose comfort over decorum."

Virginia stepped up to Wolf carrying two wine glasses and handed him one. "It shouldn't be more than an hour. My father will let me know the time of his arrival."

"He's coming by boat, isn't he?" Bacon asked.

"Who told you that?"

Bacon thumbed at Wolf. "Your boyfriend. We had long talk yesterday about the logistics of this sale."

Virginia glared at Wolf.

He shrugged. *I didn't know that was a secret. Geesh. She should have told me to keep that to myself.*

"Have a seat, Virginia. Relax." Bacon waved toward the other wicker chair next to the desk.

She drifted in that direction, lowered herself onto the seat and placed her shoulder bag beside it. Wolf noticed a stool next to the wicker chair and sat on it.

Underdonk glanced out the window. "Do you think your father will dock the boat over here at the Shallowbag Bay Marina?"

Virginia placed the glass of wine on the desk. "I don't know. It's hard to say where my father will park the boat. It's a big island."

"He won't park over there," Bacon said. It's too public. I've known him a long time. We have similar interests — history, antiques and calculated gambles. One thing I know for sure, Thomas Ellis doesn't like increasing his odds."

"Where do you think he'll dock it?" Underdock asked.

Bacon clasped his hands behind his head. "I could take an educated guess, but it really doesn't matter, does it?"

"Not really," Wolf said. "I'm the only one authorized to pick up the diary. Wherever he decides to come to shore, I'll meet him, retrieve the heirloom and deliver it safely here."

"I hope you are trustworthy, Mr. Wolf," Underdonk said.

"I'm more trustworthy than a golden retriever." Wolf cleared his throat. "I'll tell you who is *not* trustworthy." He pointed toward the stairs and shifted his eyes to Bacon. "Your nephew Willard. If he follows me, I'll snuff him out before he can send up the sinner's prayer."

Bacon waved dismissively. "Oh, don't worry about Willard."

"Bullshit. I've lost count of the number of times he's threatened to kill me. When we got here, he was loading a Ruger revolver. I stepped to go past him, and he pointed the gun at me. Right here." Wolf pointed to the middle of his chest. "Right where he shot Fregiotto."

Bacon raised his hand and patted the air. "Take it easy. He's brash and a little reckless, but he'll do what I tell him to do."

Wolf jabbed his finger at Bacon. "I'm telling you! If he follows me, I'll blow his head off and claim self-defense. Wolf waved across the room. "And Virginia doesn't want him up here when I'm gone."

"Okay!" Bacon growled. "We get it! You're the tough guy. You make the rules. I'll tell him to stay on the porch while you're getting the diary. If he follows you, go ahead and shoot him."

"That's better." Wolf took a long swig of wine.

"Did you bring his gun?" Bacon asked.

Wolf wiped his mouth with the back of his hand. "You'll get the gun back if you win the auction. Like I told you, I'm keeping it if you lose."

Bacon grunted.

"That's not fair," Underdonk pouted. "That gun is evidence in a homicide."

"So," Wolf said.

"Now Alfred has more incentive to spend the Mob's money."

"Shut your face!" Bacon ordered. "Money is money. I have my backers. I'll bid what I want to bid. Who cares where I get the money?"

"Amen," Wolf chimed, "and I hope both of you have plenty."

Underdonk stood. "How high are you willing to go to save your nephew's life?"

Bacon lowered his eyebrows. "You'll find out."

Underdonk straightened his suit jacket. "I should walk out of here right now. The deck is stacked against me."

A wide smile broke across Bacon's face. "There's the door. I won't stop you."

Wolf's heart ratcheted up a few beats. *Crap. I hope that pipsqueak doesn't turn and waddle out of here like a miffed penguin. This could fall apart fast.*

Underdonk glanced from face to face, and an unusual calm flowed over his agitated state. His head bobbed slowly. A strange smile widened his thin mustache. "No. I think I'll stay." He sat down daintily and crossed his legs. "I *want* to make Mr. Bacon spend the Mob's money. We'll see how high he's willing to go."

Bacon sat up, spun across the bed and stomped his leather slippers on the floor with a muffled thump. "You better only bid what you are willing and able to pay."

Underdonk smiled derisively. "I'll bid what I want to bid."

Forming a fist with his right hand, Bacon growled, "I ought to knock you right through that window."

Underdonk fished his small handgun out of his jacket pocket and with jerky movements, managed to aim it at Bacon. "Temper, temper, Alfred, or you won't be begging *any* money from those Charlotte goodfellas."

"Gentlemen, please," Virginia pleaded. "You're acting like kindergarten kids fighting over a Dr. Seuss book."

"Ha!" Wolf blurted out and stood. "I don't like green eggs and Bacon. I would not like him here or there. I would not like him anywhere. I would not like him, Virginia Dare."

All three turned and stared at Wolf as if he had lost his mind.

He clapped his hands. "C'mon! That's a damn good rhyme. I'm just trying to break up the tension here. Laugh a little, huh?"

Underdonk giggled. "I sorta liked it." He slipped his gun back into his pocket.

Wolf slapped his knee. "See! Mr. Purple Pants has a sense of humor."

A laugh rumbled up deep from Bacon's chest. He swung his legs onto the bed and scooted back against the pillows. His laugh burst out like a Tommy Gun but then stopped abruptly. "You should be on that show."

"What show?" Wolf asked. "America's Got Talent?"

"No. The Gong Show." The mirth had gone out of Bacon's tone. "I would have gonged you before you finished the poem."

"The Gong Show?" Wolf said. "That show hasn't been on in decades. That's an old school show, Mr. Bacon."

"I know." His voice sounded like a truck dumping gravel. "I'm old school. I believe in the old way of doing things—the code of honor. Keep your contracts. Fulfill your promises."

The room became deadly quiet for a few interminable seconds. In the silence, from Wolf's pants came a noticeable "ding!" He dipped his hand into his front pocket and slid out his cell phone. With his thumb he pressed the ID button and tapped on the text message icon. The latest one was from Angie: *We're at the Shaddai Restaurant. The silver Cascada just drove by with Gatsby Boy at the wheel heading north. Just thought you might want to know.*

Wolf glowered at Bacon. "Where did Willard run off to?"

"What?"

"You heard me."

Bacon shrugged. "As far as I know, he's right outside."

"You're wrong. My assistant just spotted his car heading north on Highway 64."

"He's a junk food addict. Maybe he went to get a burger and fries. You didn't tell me to chain him to the back porch."

Wolf gazed out the window. *What's happening here? He's up to something. Could Bacon know where Ellis is going to dock the boat? I doubt it. But . . . he could make a good guess — a calculated gamble.* He sucked in a quick breath. *Now what do I do? Try to go after him? That wouldn't be smart. It'd be a wild goose chase.*

"Oh no," Virginia gasped.

Wolf shifted his focus to her. She stared at her phone.

"My father sent me a text about ten minutes ago, but I didn't notice. I had my volume turned down."

Wolf leaned in her direction. "Let me see it."

She held up the phone, and Wolf read the message: *Arriving in about fifteen minutes. Old dock beyond the woods at the northern tip of the island near Elizabethan Gardens and Fort Raleigh. The exact spot where our ancestors came ashore. Send your man.*

"Do you know where that is?" she asked.

"I know exactly where that is."

"You better get going."

Wolf glared at Bacon. "I hope you're right about your nephew. Big Macs and fries kill slowly, but a well-aimed bullet kills instantly."

Bacon grinned like a sly crocodile. "Didn't you hear what the lady said? You better get going."

He hustled toward the steps, hurried down them two at a time, and rushed out the bottom door and across the breezeway. Willard had vanished, but where did he go? Wolf sprinted across the lawn and onto the street. He threw open the car door and leapt into the Cougar. He started the engine and backed away from the Jaguar. Ahead he could see the empty space where the Cascada had been parked in front of the Rolls Royce. He peeled out and sped down the street to the stop sign, made a left on Lord Essex Avenue and another left on Ananias Dare Street, which led back to Route 64. *Don't panic yet. Maybe Willard is a junk-food junkie.* The more he thought about it, though, the less it made sense. *Alfred told Willard to keep his eye out for any suspicious people loitering around the back of the inn. If that were his assignment, he'd obey orders. Alfred must have issued new orders. He's not at the McDonald's drive-thru. He's on a mission to get to that boat.*

Wolf stopped at the light and checked for oncoming traffic. Seeing none, he hit the accelerator and turned right onto Highway 64, the tires sliding and then gripping the road. He remembered that the Shaddai Restaurant was back a few blocks. Willard must have headed south first to check the Shallowbag Bay Marina just in case Uncle Alfred's guess was wrong. After a quick inspection, he drove north on 64. That's when Angie spotted him. If that's the case, he's got about a ten-minute head start.

Angie was incredible. Out on her first date with a good-looking young deputy, and yet she still had the mindfulness and observational skills to recognize Willard's car when it flew past. *Geesh! That girl is a natural.* Wolf caught sight of a speed limit sign — 35 mph. He pushed the Cougar to 50 but kept it there because of the possibility of cars pulling out of side streets and driveways. The road ran right through the middle of Manteo and all its small-town neighborhoods. *Yessiree, Angie has what it takes. Who knows what direction my life will go? Maybe I will hire her on as my partner, . . . if I don't end up getting myself killed.*

About a mile from downtown, the houses and stores thinned out, replaced by patches of woods and an occasional church. Old Fort Raleigh and the Elizabethan Gardens were less than two miles away. How much did Alfred Bacon know?

Wolf remembered his words when he ruminated about Thomas Ellis and where he might dock the boat. Bacon had said he knew Ellis well and shared a love of history and antiques with him. When Wolf had met with him yesterday, Bacon confirmed that he saw the Dare Diary in person and had checked out the scientific and archeological reports on its authenticity. Perhaps he and Ellis discussed the history of colonists—where they landed on the island near Old Fort Raleigh and how they survived those first few years. *No doubt about it. Bacon is smarter than he looks. He knows how to read between the lines. Ellis and he probably talked at length about the circumstances surrounding the fate the colonists.* The closer Wolf drew to the Elizabethan Gardens, the more he was convinced that Alfred Bacon's educated guess was spot on.

He turned right onto Fort Raleigh Road. The tall pines and oaks cast their early afternoon shadows across his windshield like a slow-motion strobe light, causing him to squint and blink. What would happen if Willard got to the boat first? Virginia had sent her father Wolf's photo for identification purposes. *Ellis would take one look at the photograph and tell him to get lost.* Wolf recalled seeing Willard loading the gun on the steps of the breezeway. *Then Willard would pull out that revolver and take the diary by force. That's exactly what would happen.* Wolf gritted his teeth. *Crap!* Bacon's plan came into Wolf's mind with crystal clarity. Once he discovered the diary would arrive by boat, he had plotted out the possibilities. *I played right into his hand.* "Dammit!" *With Willard banished from the upper room, he'd be free to carry out his uncle's orders—find the boat, swipe the diary and get the hell out of town. I've got to stop him.*

Up ahead Wolf saw the Fort Raleigh Visitor Center where he had parked yesterday. About fifteen parking spaces lined the road to the right of the building. Three cars sat in the first few spaces on the left nearest the center. The Silver Cascada occupied the last space on the far right. Wolf pulled in next to the Cascada and sprang out of the car. He headed toward the flowering bush and thicket of trees where the path to the dock began. *Willard knew right where to go. He and Alfred must have done some reconnaissance yesterday.* Wolf cut into the shadows between the bush and the trees.

He proceeded along the weed-patched path cautiously, keeping his eyes focused on the myriad flecks of light and shifting organic shades. At any second he anticipated seeing Willard's form materialize from the depths of tangled underbrush. He lifted his shirt, unsnapped his holster and drew out his handgun. After advancing a little more than a hundred yards he came to the Y in the path where he had encountered the rattlesnake. He turned onto the left trail, walked a few steps and stopped. *If Ellis moored the boat to that old dock, then I'm less than two hundred yards away.* He saw movement and crouched. Above the mottling of bushes and vines he spied the Gatsby cap bobbing with every step. He crawled backwards to the split in the trail. Glancing behind him, he spotted a large live oak not far along the other path. Carefully he edged backwards and pressed himself against the trunk of the other side of the tree.

Footsteps increased in volume. Willard emerged through the snarled greenery carrying an old wooden box about the size of a medium suitcase. He turned onto the path toward the visitor center. Wolf stood and watched him from behind. The handle of the Ruger revolver stuck out of the back of his pants. Wolf raised his pistol, aimed at the middle of Willard's back and strode toward him.

"Gatsby Boy," Wolf called.

Willard froze.

"Turn around and let me see the golden egg."

He turned slowly and glared at Wolf, his face fraught with hostility.

"I have to give your uncle some credit. He's smarter than the average crook."

"A lot smarter than asswipes like you," he hissed.

"If that were true, I wouldn't be here ready to blow a hole through your brain."

He raised the box to block his head. "Don't shoot the golden egg. It's priceless."

"Would you rather I blast your nuts off?"

Willard lowered the box.

"How much of a price did Thomas Ellis pay after he handed it over? Did he pay with his life?"

A dubious smile cracked Willard's face. "You got it all wrong, Blue-Light Boy. Ellis knows Uncle Alfred and me. We're old friends. He handed the diary over without a question. He said he trusted me more than you to deliver it."

"That's a lie. How many bullets do you have left in your revolver?"

"Don't worry. I've got enough left for you."

Wolf hooked his finger toward his chest several times. "Come here and turn around. This is getting to be a habit-- taking guns away from you."

He plodded toward Wolf to within a couple feet.

"If you did kill Ellis or Fregiotto, I'll make sure *you* pay the price."

Willard thrust the wooden box forward. It slammed into Wolf's chest and face, knocking him to the ground. His gun tumbled into the weeds. As he struggled to his feet, Willard reached behind himself and fumbled for the revolver. Wolf dove at him. Williard whipped the gun around and fired. The bullet whizzed by Wolf's ear just before he collided with Willard. They hit the ground and skidded against a thick tree trunk. The kid was wiry but strong. He tried to break away by rolling and kicking, but Wolf was too big. Then he tried to pistol whip him but only could manage a few glancing blows. Wolf snagged his gun hand and began beating it against the tree trunk. The revolver broke loose and landed by Wolf's leg. He planted his knees next to Willard's armpits and pinned his hands to the ground. Willard pummeled Wolf's back by kicking up his knees.

"Stop it!" Wolf ordered.

Willard kept kicking.

Wolf let go of one hand and slapped him hard across the face.

Now that his hand was free, Willard tried to reach for the pistol.

"That's how you want to play, huh?" Wolf said. He reached back, snatched the revolver from beside his leg and raised it above his head. Willard's free hand waved in front of his face, trying to block the blow. Wolf brought the grip of the gun down hard. Willard partially blocked it, but it still struck him above his right eye. Willard blinked, panic engulfing his face. Wolf raised the gun and slammed it down again. Willard's block missed, and the handle smashed into the middle of his forehead. Blood strteamed from the gash as his head fell backwards. His eyes rolled up, the irises disappearing. Wolf breathed hard but tried to remain still, waiting to detect any movement. Willard lay there like a burlap sack filled with rotten apples. He was out cold.

Wolf got to his feet and checked Willard's revolver. It was a seven shooter. *Two bullets left.* He shook his head, wondering if Thomas Ellis took the other four slugs. He secured the revolver between his belt and pants. Looking left and right, he scoured the ground where he had fallen. He spotted his pistol under a bush, dropped to his knees and picked it up. After rising to his feet, he walked back to the body. Willard's chest rose and fell slowly. *He's not dead. I guess that's good news.*

Wolf trudged over to the wooden box and picked it up. It was surprisingly big and heavy considering its contents. *Must be well secured and packed tight like a pharaoh's coffin.* He hurried along the path and broke through the opening into the sunshine. Glancing around, he noticed a heavyset guy standing in front of the Fort Raleigh Visitor Center, smoking a cigarette and wearing black-framed sunglasses. Dressed in a Hawaiian shirt, yellow shorts and sandals, the guy watched him approach the Cougar. Wolf swung open the passenger's side door and lowered the box onto the seat. Keeping his back to tourist, he eased Willard's revolver out from his belt and placed it into the glove compartment. Then he swung the door shut, turned and nodded at the man.

The tourist smiled and waved. "How ya doing, buddy?"

Wolf hustled back to the path and into the shadows. He jogged, quickly covering the hundred yards to Willard's body. He bent over and examined Willard's face. *Still out cold.* The Gatsby cap lay in the weeds a few feet away. *Don't want to forget that.* He swiped the hat off the ground and dropped it onto Willard's chest. Then he grabbed him by the ankles and, walking backwards, dragged him along the trail. Willard wore low cut oiled work boots with heavy treads, which made it easier to hold on to him. The blood had stopped oozing, but a huge lump had formed on his forehead. All the jostling didn't stir him into consciousness one bit. When he reached the opening, he peeked out and saw the guy still smoking away. *What am I going to do now? What the hell? I can't waste time. I'll come up with something.*

He plowed forward by walking backwards and dragging the body into the sunshine. By the time he reached the back of the Cougar, the smoker had noticed. With great alarm clouding his features, the tourist approached the car. Wolf let go of Willard's ankles, and the work shoes thudded on the asphalt. He quickly drew his keys out of his pocket and opened the trunk.

"Is everything okay?" the man asked in a high-pitched voice.

"Oh yeah." Wolf smiled and waved at Willard's body. "My buddy got drunk and took a tumble in the woods."

"That's quite a knot on his head."

"He must have fallen hard. I'm going to take him home and put an ice pack on his noggin."

The guy lowered his sunglasses. "Are you going to put him in the trunk?"

Wolf nodded. "I don't trust him when he wakes up from one these benders. He can get violent. He'll be fine in the trunk. Plenty of air flow back here. Hey, could you help me out and grab his feet."

The man eyed Willard's shoes, frowned and then refocused on Wolf. "Are you serious?"

"As serious as a TV preacher selling prayer cloths."

"Well . . . I guess I could lend a hand."

"Thanks, brother!"

Wolf circled the body and cupped Willard around the armpits. The heavyset guy grasped his ankles and lifted his legs. Wolf counted to three, and they heaved the body into the trunk with an unsettling thurrummp! The backend of the car seesawed for a few seconds.

Wolf reached to close the trunk."

"Wait a minute, buddy," the tourist said.

Wolf froze.

The heavyset guy bent over and picked up the Gatsby cap off the asphalt. "Does this belong to him?"

Wolf smiled like a used car salesman. "That's his favorite hat. Just toss it in there."

With a flick of the wrist, the guy lobbed the hat and it alighted on Willard's butt.

"Perfect landing." Wolf slammed the trunk shut and winked at the man. "Thanks again, brother, and I'll tell my buddy what a big help you were."

He wiped beads of sweat off his forehead and said, "I sure hope your friend will be alright."

"Ahhhhh." Wolf gave a nonchalant wave. "He'll be fine."

Wolf climbed into the front seat, started the engine and drove off.

Chapter 20

As Wolf cruised down Highway 64, the thought of Thomas Ellis lying dead in that boat haunted him. Willard had denied killing him, but the Ruger revolver told a different story—two bullets left in the cylinder. Where were the other five? One of them almost took off Wolf's ear. If the other four were lodged in Ellis's chest, Wolf couldn't do much about it. Could Ellis have survived? Very doubtful, although Wolf felt a twinge of guilt for not checking on him. That would have taken another fifteen or twenty minutes. By then, Willard may have stirred back to life and escaped. *I can't cover all the bases. Hopefully, he's alive. If not, he's a casualty of graft and greed. I should have never told Bacon the diary was arriving by boat. Little mistakes beget big troubles.*

Wolf glanced at the old wooden box on the seat next to him. Now the question was how to approach the sale. *Do I tell them Willard's out in my trunk? Hell no. I've got to play it cool. Who knows what happened to Willard? Maybe he fell asleep in a booth at McDonald's. Maybe he choked on a Big Mac.* Wolf took in a deep breath and let it out with a low whistle. *I'll handle this as if nothing went wrong. I boarded the boat. Mr. Ellis made sure my face matched the ID photo. We talked for a few minutes. He handed over the diary. I told him I'd see him after the sale and left.* Confidence slowly arose within him. He'd take one step at a time and make the best decisions moment by moment.

Sooner or later, though, the big moment would come. In that moment the fate of these players on this bizarre stage would be determined. Would that moment bring wealth and romance? Or would it bring truth and justice? One outcome offered freedom from the grind of making a living in a corrupt world; the other offered the challenge of building a business of dealing with the world's corruption. Could he do both?

Could he reap the riches by pulling off the sale and then turn over the evidence against Willard and Alfred Bacon? That would be difficult. They would squeal like pigs in the slaughterhouse yard. There would be lawsuits concerning the stolen diary and perhaps criminal charges. That's the chance he would have to take to go for gold.

As he neared town he heard sirens. A few hundred yards ahead a large red firetruck turned onto Highway 64. Wolf hit his brakes and slowed to about fifteen mph as the vehicle flew by. An ambulance, red with white stripes, and another firetruck followed close behind. Their whirling lights triggered a spate of whirling thoughts in Wolf's mind. *They're heading toward the north end of the island. It's probably a house fire or vehicle accident. I'd bet on those odds.* That probability didn't hamper the possibilities that continued to swirl in his mind. *Maybe someone found Thomas Ellis. Maybe he crawled out of that boat onto that old dock and yelled for help.* The image of the heavyset tourist appeared on the screen of his mind. *Could he have heard or seen something? He knew where I entered the woods. The sound of someone yelling would have come from that direction. Maybe Ellis staggered through the woods, calling for help, and the guy heard him. Don't get carried away! Deal with what you know to be true.* Wolf took several calming breaths. In that moment he came to a decision.

He turned right onto Budleigh Street and parked behind Underdonk's Jaguar. After cutting the engine, he turned and listened to see if he could hear any rustling from the trunk. Silence. He pulled his cell phone out of his jeans pocket, pressed his thumb on the ID button, and activated the phone. Scrolling through his contacts, he found Angie's number and hit the call button.

It rang twice. "Hello."

"Angie, this is Wes."

"I know. I can read my caller ID."

"I need your help."

"What's up?"

"Is Deputy Thomas still with you?"

"Yeah."

"Good. I've got Gatsby Boy in my trunk."

There was a pause. "I don't think I heard you correctly."

"You heard me alright. I've got Gatsby Boy in my trunk. I'm parked in front of the Cameron House Inn."

"What's he doing in your trunk?"

"Sleeping peacefully. I'll explain in more detail later."

"What do you want me to do?"

"Get over here as soon as you can. Tell Joel to call Sheriff Walton and meet you there."

"What do I do with Gatsby Boy when I get there?"

"Leave him in the trunk until Walton arrives. Tell Walton I've got the gun that Willard Bacon used to kill Fregiotto. He needs to arrest him on suspicion of murder. I'll put the keys under my floormat."

"I hope he believes me."

"If he doesn't, tell him Willard may have killed someone else, too."

"Who?"

"Thomas Ellis. I'm not sure about that yet, but it's a good possibility."

"Okay. I'll do my best to convince him."

"Once they haul Gastby Boy out of there, wait until Underdonk and Bacon leave the annex building behind the inn. Their cars are parked in front of mine. Tell Joel not to let them get away. They need to be questioned about these homicides. Underdonk is a witness, and Bacon is a possible accomplice."

"What about Virginia Dare? You need to question her."

"I know. She'll be with me. I'll find out what we need to know from her."

"Okay, Big Boss Man, I'll take care of it."

"Angel . . . "

"Yeah?"

"I'm counting on you."

"I've got your back."

When Wolf tucked the phone back into his pocket, he heard a groan. He sat quietly for a few seconds. *Go back to dreamland, Willard.* He slipped the keys under the floor mat, got out of the car, circled to the passenger side door and opened it. Tilting his head, he listened again. Silence. He picked up the wooden box, closed the door gently and shuffled to the back of the car. No groans. No movement. *Sweet dreams, Gatsby Boy. When you wake up, the nightmare begins.*

Wolf hurried across the lawn to the annex building at the back of the inn. He trotted up the few steps and crossed the breezeway. Cradling the box in his left arm, he opened the door and sidled into the entryway. Before heading up the stairs, he checked his watch—1:13. He had been gone for almost forty-five minutes. It seemed like three hours. Hopefully, all was well upstairs: no bickering, no cane thumping, no code of honor vengeance. Wolf mounted the steps with his fingers crossed.

When he walked into the bedroom, all three of them stood as if he were carrying the Holy Grail.

"Is that it?" Underdonk said. "Is that the Dare Diary?"

"I presume it is, but we won't know for sure until we take off the lid and examine the contents."

They approached slowly, Bacon from the other side of the far bed, and Underdonk and Virginia from their wicker chairs.

Wolf lowered the weathered box onto the closest bed.

"What took so long?" Virginia asked.

"I've only been gone about forty minutes. It seemed like an eternity because you were stuck here with these two devils."

Bacon appeared confused. "Where's Willard?"

Wolf scowled at Bacon. "Were you expecting Willard to arrive with the diary?"

"Of course not."

"I didn't think so."

"I just wondered what happened to him. Is he outside on the steps?"

"I didn't see him out there. You said he had a junk food addiction. Maybe he overdosed at McDonalds."

Bacon grunted.

"Who cares what happened to Willard?" Underdonk panted like an old dog on a hot afternoon. "Let's examine the diary."

"Back off," Wolf commanded. "Let's get a few things straight before we tear off the lid."

"What do you mean?" Underdonk barked. "We've already agreed to your conditions. We've been waiting here for close to an hour. Let's get on with the auction."

Wolf held out his hands placatingly. "I just want to refresh your memories."

"Your wasting our time," Bacon growled. "Let's look at the diary and get the bidding started."

Wolf glanced out the window, wondering if Angie and Joel had arrived yet. It might take ten or fifteen minutes for the sheriff to get here. "Patience! I'm running this show. We're going to go over my rules."

Underdonk crossed his arms, and Bacon protruded his lower lip, but they remained silent. Virginia gazed at Wolf with questioning eyes. Wolf covered all the details he had gone over when he had met with them individually: the bidding would start at twenty million; the diary would not be handed over until the funds were transferred; neither the winner nor loser would ever disclose the identity of the sellers; if Bacon won the auction, Wolf would return Willard's gun; if he didn't, Wolf would keep the gun to insure Bacon's pledge of confidentiality. He went over each point in painstaking detail. When he finished, he smiled and scanned their faces.

Bacon lowered his thick eyebrows. "Are you finished?"

Wolf rubbed his hands together. "I think I've covered it all. Is everyone in full agreement?"

Bacon and Underdonk nodded begrudgingly.

Virginia smiled, the corners of her mouth twitching. "Yes."

"Good." Wolf wiped his palm downward over his face. "Before I open the box, I need to get a breath of fresh air. I'm feeling a little out of sorts." He walked around the beds to the other side of the room."

"Are you sick?" Virginia asked.

"A little queasy." Wolf raised the window and stuck his head out. He peered to the right and spotted Joel's white Ford F150 parked behind his car. He didn't see the sheriff's vehicle, but Angie and Joel stood next to the Cougar gazing at the trunk. Taking a deep breath, he murmured, "Come on, Walton, what's taking so long?"

"Did you say something?" Virginia asked.

Wolf drew back from the window. "Yes. I needed that fresh air. I feel much better now."

"Then open the damn box," Bacon growled.

Wolf sauntered back to the bed, edged around Bacon's girth and cut in between Underdonk and Virginia. The top of the box resembled weathered barn siding, about two feet by two and a half feet with a latch on each side. One by one, he flipped up the latches. The three onlookers leaned closer. He lifted the lid and let it fall onto the other side of the bed. A musty smell arose from the contents. The inside of the box was stuffed with what appeared to be scraps of an old quilt. Wolf picked up one of the scraps and held it in front of his face. It was about the size of a hand towel. He threw it to the side.

Underdonk reached to remove another strip, but Wolf caught his hand and said, "Stay back! I'll handle this."

"I was just trying to help," Underdonk whined.

"No one touches anything until the funds have been transferred. Got it?"

Underdonk gave a half-hearted salute. "Whatever you say, Sarge."

"Quit stalling," Bacon said. "I'm in a hurry."

Wolf straightened and thumbed over his shoulder. "If you don't have the patience for this, there's the door."

Bacon's face flushed. "I'd like to take a ball bat and . . . and . . ."

"And what?" Wolf said.

"Never mind." He motioned toward the box. "C'mon. Remove the stuffing."

Wolf took his time clearing away the quilted cloth. An ancient leather book cover gradually appeared. It had a leather strap around the middle with a primitive buckle. Once all the strips had be removed, Wolf said, "Virginia, I'm going to lift the diary. When I do, slide the box out of the way to the other side of the bed."

Virginia nodded nervously. "Okay. Go ahead. I'm ready."

With delicate movements, Wolf slid his fingers under the bottom of the diary and lifted it carefully. Virginia crouched and pushed the box to the other side of the bed. She eased backwards out of the way. Wolf lowered the diary onto the beige bedspread and removed his hands.

"There it is, boys," Wolf said, "the Dare Diary."

Underdonk stared at it and wheezed audibly, his chest heaving up and down.

Bacon's red face lost its color as his eyes widened.

Wolf pointed to the top of the leather cover. "This artifact . . . this heirloom . . . this relic . . . this historical treasure is about to make one of you incredibly rich. Are we ready to begin the bidding? Who will open with twenty million?"

"Not so fast," Bacon grumbled. "I want to examine the pages."

"Of course," Wolf said. He cautiously slid the strap through the old buckle and placed it to the side of the diary. Carefully, he lifted the ancient cover and lowered it onto the bedspread. The first page, discolored with age and its edges slightly ragged, was blank. With his thumb and forefinger, Wolf delicately pinched the corner of the page and drew it slowly back. The second page was blank.

"Keep going," Underdonk said.

Page by page, Wolf went through the diary, picking up his pace as he progressed, but the pages were all blank.

Bacon pivoted and glared at Virginia. "What's going on here?"

Her eyes widened, and her lower lip quivered. She grasped Wolf's elbow. "Did my father hand this box to you?"

Wolf knew something had went wrong. Now what? The truth or a lie? It didn't matter. The auction ended before it started. "No. I ran into Willard along the path in the woods as I was heading to the dock. We fought, and I knocked him out. I picked up the box and assumed it was the real deal."

Virginia's head wagged back and forth. "Noooo! Father would never hand the authentic diary to an imposter. He had your photograph on his phone to check the receiver's identification. My father always plans ahead. He had prepared a bogus diary just in case something like this happened."

Bacon stepped closer. "Are you saying the real diary is still on the boat?"

"Yes. It's still on the boat with my father."

Bacon whirled and marched toward the stairs. Underdonk gave each of them a quick glance, edged around Wolf and went after Bacon.

"Where are they going?" Virginia asked.

"To your father's boat to steal the diary."

"Shouldn't we follow them?"

"No."

"Why not?"

"They won't get very far."

"What do you mean?"

Wolf took her hand and led her to the window. The sheriff's car and another cruiser had arrived. A few seconds later several deputies surrounded Underdonk and Bacon as they walked toward their cars.

Virginia inhaled and beathed out haltingly. "This is a total mess. Will they be arrested?"

"That's a good possibility. I've got the murder weapon that killed Fregiotto. Bacon is an accomplice, and Underdonk knows what happened. They'll question both of them thoroughly."

"Maybe it's all for the best." She turned away from the window.

"Why do you say that?"

"Those two chiselers were risky bets. You saw what just happened. As soon as they found out about the real diary, they wanted to steal it. Knowing my father, he wouldn't hang around that dock anyway. He probably set sail as soon as Willard left with the forgery. He'll go into hiding and see what happens. Sooner or later he'll find a buyer."

"Don't count on that."

Virginia gave Wolf an apprehensive frown. "Why not?"

"Do you remember the first person we saw when we got here?"

"Willard."

"That's right. What was he doing?"

Her face muscles tensed. "He was loading his gun."

Wolf nodded. "When I ran into him in the woods, he fired once at me. I managed to disarm him and knock him out with his own revolver. It was a seven shooter. When I checked the cylinder, there were only two bullets left."

She clamped her hands to the sides of her head. "Do you think he shot my father . . . f-f-four times?"

"I'm not sure, but that's my best guess."

She collapsed into his arms and sobbed. He rubbed her back soothingly as she wept for several minutes. When her sniffling subsided, he grasped her shoulders and pushed her away slightly. "My best guess could be wrong."

"Let's hope so." Her dark eyes met his. "Kiss me."

Wolf kissed her passionately, their bodies seeming to meld together. They broke apart, and she caressed his cheek. He kissed her forehead and the tip of her nose. Their lips reunited, and mouths opened, their tongues touching, feeling, desperately seeking. In the midst of their intimate connection, Virginia broke away abruptly.

"We need to get going," she said.

"Where?"

"If Willard killed my father, the diary is still on the boat. No one knows about it yet except for Underdonk and Bacon. We'll get the diary and go back to my place in Charlotte. I know we can find the right buyers. We'll make a fortune. After we sell it, we can move out of the country, go to the Bahamas or maybe the South Pacific. We can be free."

"Slow down." Wolf took a step back. "There're some questions that need to be answered."

"What questions?"

"For example: What will the Bacons and Underdonk tell the authorities?"

Her eyes lost their focus on him. "They'll snitch. They'll say my father stole the diary."

"None of them have any incentive to cover for you, especially the Bacons. They're headed to jail on murder charges."

She refocused on Wolf. "But we can fight those accusations in court. That diary belongs to my family. A jury will side with me."

"You may be right. That's another question yet to be answered." Wolf took another step back.

Her pale face reddened, and she edged toward him. "If you love me, you'll stand by me no matter what happens."

Inching backwards, Wolf bumped into the nightstand. "Virginia, I will stand by you, but I need to make sure I'm standing on solid ground. I learned something recently that raises another question in my mind."

She straightened, the flames in her eyes dying. "What . . . what are you . . . talking about?"

"When I visited Laura Bain last night, she told me something that overrides everything that has happenbed. She said that when George left the house on the night he was murdered, she followed him."

"What does that have to do with us?"

"She said a tall woman approached his car as he sat outside of Fregiotto's beach house. He got out of the car, and they went for a walk. She became angry and drove away in the opposite direction. She couldn't identify the woman."

Her eyes caught fire again. "That wasn't me!"

"That's good to hear, but I need proof."

"Don't you believe me? How can I prove it?"

Wolf pointed toward the wicker chair. "Hand over that .38 special you've got tucked in your purse. The pathologist pulled a .38 slug out of George's heart. If it doesn't match up with your gun, then you're in the clear."

She took a step backwards. "That's not a problem. You can have the gun." She glanced over her shoulder at her leather bag next to the chair. "I'll get it for you." She rushed to the shoulder bag, opened it and fumbled inside. She stood, spun toward Wolf and raised the gun. Her hand trembled.

Wolf took in a sharp breath. "Put the gun down, Virginia."

She shook her head. "I had to kill your partner."

"Why?"

"I knew they would arrest Frank for his murder."

Wolf nodded. "I see. You wanted Frank out of the way, which would also eliminate Underdonk."

"That's right. Without Frank, Underdonk had no inroad. Eliminating Underdonk would appease Alfred."

"But then Willard killed Fregiotto, and I was drawn into this mess."

"Yes." Her chin quivered. "And you brought Underdonk back into the mix. But then I . . . I . . . I fell in love with you."

"If you love me, put the gun down."

Her head shook like a kid facing the doctor's needle. "You're not going to put me in jail. I'd never survive in prison." She steadied the pistol.

"Drop the gun!" a woman's voice commanded.

Virginia whirled and fired.

A loud blast followed. Virginia flew backwards, her pistol twirling through the air. Her body thudded onto the floor beside the far bed, and the pistol landed on the other bed next to the phony diary.

Wolf charged forward and peered around the corner. Angie stood at the top of the stairs, holding her Smith and Wesson handgun. Her wide eyes met Wolf's. She breathed rapidly. A bullet hole marred the wall about six inches above her head.

"I had to shoot her!" she wailed.

"I know."

"She was going to kill you."

"You had my back."

Angie lowered the gun and walked toward the body. Wolf followed. Virginia's eyes, frozen in an agonized stare, glared at Wolf. Her arms lay at odd angles, her legs spread. The bullet had ripped a large hole in the middle of her chest, the blood seeping and spreading on her white blouse into a ragged heart shape.

Chapter 21

Angie drifted over and sat on the far bed. "I feel sick." She placed the gun on the bedspread and slid it away from her.

"Take deep breaths, Angel. You're in shock," Wolf sat down next to her. He couldn't define how he felt inside. It was an odd feeling as if he had just awakened from an erotic dream that suddenly turned into a nightmare. He felt the sadness of loss and the joy of being alive at the same time.

She closed her eyes and breathed long, controlled breaths for a couple minutes.

Wolf leaned and examined her pale face. "Are you okay?"

She nodded. "I'm sorry I killed your girlfriend."

Wolf shrugged. "I don't think it would have worked out anyway."

"Not if you were dead."

"Death *is* a dealbreaker."

She patted his knee. "You better call the emergency squad and get the coroner up here."

Wolf pulled out his phone. "It may take them a while. They were heading north on 64 when I was coming back into town."

"We heard the sirens. Sounded serious."

"Yeah. A couple firetrucks and an ambulance."

Angie thumbed toward the window. "We could have used an ambulance out there."

"Why? What happened?"

"Once Sheriff Walton arrived, I opened the trunk. Willard looked like an extra from the *Walking Dead*."

"Was he conscious?"

Angie nodded. "He said he couldn't see straight, and his head hurt like he just drank a 7/11 Cherry Freeze."

"I might have cracked his skull."

"That would explain it."

Wolf called 911 and requested an ambulance and a coroner. He gave them the Cameron House Inn address and told them to get there as soon as possible.

He patted her knee. "You'll have to stay here and answer questions."

"I know. Sheriff Walton said he's coming up to talk to you as soon as he takes care of business down there."

"Good ol' Sheriff Walton. I'm sure he'll offer me some high praise for doing his job for him."

"No doubt." Angie glanced over her shoulder at Virginia's body. "Was she the woman Laura saw with George?"

Wolf nodded. "Yep. They took a walk on the beach, and she shot him in the heart with that same gun she aimed at me."

Angie swallowed. "The same one she fired at me."

Wolf pointed to the .38 special on the other bed. "That's the murder weapon."

"Is that the Dare Diary next to it?"

"No. That's a forgery."

"Do you mean to tell me . . ." Her eyes narrowed. ". . . that people lost their lives over something that wasn't even real?"

Footfalls thudded up the steps with increasing volume. They raised their heads to see Deputy Thomas enter the room.

He froze and stared at Virginia's body. "Is that . . . is that your girlfriend, Wes? Emma Ritz?"

Wolf stood, ambled toward the body and stopped a few feet away. He took a deep breath and let it out audibly. "Her name was Virginia Dare. She entered my life unexpectedly a few days ago. I thought we were falling in love."

"I'm so sorry, Wes. What happened?"

"She tried to kill me, but my guardian angel saved my life."

Deputy Thomas glanced at Angie. "You shot her?"

Angie nodded.

Wolf shook his head. "They say love comes uninvited."

"And so does death." Angie arose and stepped next to Wolf. "I don't believe she loved you one bit."

"Why do you say that, Angel?"

"You knew she had that gun and trusted her to give it to you."

"I did."

"She violated that trust. Love would never do that because love is trust."

Wolf bobbed his head slowly, reached and hugged Angie around the shoulders. "Those are words from a woman wise beyond her years."

Deputy Thomas turned from the body and faced Wolf. "Did you call for an ambulance yet? It might take a while to get here. There was a fire on the north end of the island. I just talked to a buddy on the E-squad. All the fire and emergency vehicles from the north and south stations are there."

"A house fire?" Wolf asked

"No. Someone torched a boat at that old dock near the Elizabethan Gardens. Everything went up in flames. The arsonist must have used an accelerant. They found a charred body inside, still unidentified."

Angie peered up at Wolf. "The work of Willard Bacon?"

Wolf nodded. "He murdered Thomas Ellis and tried to destroy all the evidence."

"Was the authentic diary on that boat?" Angie asked.

218

"I'm afraid it was. America's greatest mystery may never be solved."

Deputy Thomas circled the bed and examined the diary. "Hey, Wes, what's this old book here. It's full of blank pages."

Angie pivoted and stepped to the other side of the bed. "It's worthless. It's just a forgery."

Wolf walked to the foot of the bed and leaned on the footboard. "Let's not look at it that way, Detective Stallone."

Angie perked up. "What did you call me?"

"You heard me alright, partner." Wolf reached and flipped the empty pages. "I would call it a story yet to be written."

THE END

Books by Joe C. Ellis

Book 2 – Weston Wolf Outer Banks Detective Series
The Singer in the Sound

Book 3 – Weston Wolf Outer Banks Detective Series
Kitty Hawk Confidential (August 2021)

Outer Banks Murder Series

These are stand-alone novels and can be read in any order.

The Healing Place (Prequel to Murder at Whalehead)
Book 1 – Murder at Whalehead
Book 2 – Murder at Hatteras
Book 3 – Murder on the Outer Banks
Book 4 – Murder at Ocracoke
Book 5 – The Treasure of Portstmouth Island

Both mystery series are available at Outer Banks bookstores and at online book retailers.